"Claire, I think those men may have been trying to kill you."

She surged to her feet and took several steps away before whirling around to face him again. "That's impossible!" she said. "I don't know anyone in Seoul. I've only been here a few weeks, for goodness sake. Look, you've obviously made some sort of error."

Luke remained seated, still trying to keep a low profile. "I'm sorry, Claire. There is no mistake."

Claire bit her lip then started over. "I appreciate your concern. You've gone above and beyond. But there's no reason anyone would want to hurt me."

Luke sighed. "Please at least consider the possibility. Don't go anywhere alone and pay attention to your surroundings…. And, if anything remotely suspicious happens, contact the hospital security guards or the police *and* the embassy."

"Yes, sir." She gave him a small smile.

His own lips turned up slightly, but he still looked frustrated. There seemed to be nothing left to say. The interview was over.

Dear Reader,

My husband and I lived in Seoul, South Korea, for three years (2008–2011). While there I volunteered at a large "orphanage" (adoption agency), which was the basis for the one depicted in the book, though the name has been changed. On any given day, between 35 and 65 newborns were housed at that location. They lived there until about two to three weeks of age, when they were sent to a foster home. Occasionally, it was obvious that one of the infants was biracial; the idea for the character of Claire came from one such tiny baby.

While in Seoul, I also volunteered for the American Red Cross unit at Yongsan Army Garrison. The character of Luke was loosely inspired by an officer stationed there. Like Luke, this young man was a graduate of the U.S. Naval Academy and "loaned" to Yongsan as an intelligence officer. Many of the situations and dealings between the South Koreans and North Koreans described in the book are based on actual circumstances. The characters, however, are fictional.

Finally, as mentioned in the story, South Korea–the Land of the Morning Calm–is a lovely and very safe country, with warm and welcoming residents. Hopefully, one day, you will have the opportunity to visit.

I hope you enjoy the story of Claire and Luke!

Melanie Mitchell

HEARTWARMING

Melanie Mitchell
The Nurse's Bodyguard

⧫HARLEQUIN® HEARTWARMING™

Recycling programs
for this product may
not exist in your area.

ISBN-13: 978-0-373-36690-3

The Nurse's Bodyguard

Copyright © 2014 by Melanie McEwen

HARLEQUIN®
™ www.Harlequin.com

Printed in U.S.A.

MELANIE MITCHELL

is a native of Texas. With her husband, Scott, Melanie
has lived in Belgium, South Korea and a number of cities
in the United States. She has traveled throughout the
U.S.A., Canada, Europe, Asia, Africa and the Middle East.
Melanie draws on her travels and work abroad to bring a
variety of settings, experiences and an understanding of
different cultures into her work.

Melanie has been a registered nurse for many years
and currently teaches nursing in the Houston area.
While she has written extensively—nursing textbooks
and articles—she recently turned to her love of romantic
suspense. *The Nurse's Bodyguard* is her second novel.

Books by Melanie Mitchell

HARLEQUIN HEARTWARMING

OUT OF THE SHADOWS

For Pamela, who inspired me to write fiction,
and Roz, my best friend from Korea.
Thank you both for your love and support.

Tell me not, in mournful numbers,
Life is but an empty dream!—
For the soul is dead that slumbers,
And things are not what they seem.

Life is real! Life is earnest!
And the grave is not its goal;
Dust thou art, to dust returnest,
Was not spoken of the soul.

Not enjoyment, and not sorrow,
Is our destined end or way;
But to act, that each to-morrow
Find us farther than to-day.

—Henry Wadsworth Longfellow
From "A Psalm of Life"

CHAPTER ONE

Seoul, South Korea

MARY CLAIRE OLSEN smiled shyly and said good-night to the security guard sitting at a large desk near the entrance of the Samsung Medical Center. Exiting through the automatic doors, she shifted her purse to her other shoulder and buttoned her white lab coat. The spring night was cool, but a little hazy, which was apparently typical for the city during April.

Having been in Seoul for a month, Claire had established a routine. The apartment she was sharing wasn't that far from the hospital. She could take the subway home—the nearest stop was only two blocks away—or she could catch a cab. Although taxis cost a little more than the subway, the silver cabs were readily available, usually clean and remarkably cheap.

Traveling by taxi often took a bit longer because traffic was heavy, but Claire was tired. It was almost eleven and she'd put in more than twelve hours at the hospital, so she decided to find a cab.

Claire headed for the street, walking through the large, well-lit parking lot. Positive memories and cheerful thoughts bounced through her mind as she wove her way among the late-model Korean or Japanese sedans and occasional SUVs. It had been a good day. Most of the children on the hematology/oncology unit were doing well with their treatments. She recalled the smiles of the children as well as the grateful expressions on the faces of their parents. Compared to that her fatigue was secondary. Nonetheless, she was looking forward to a hot shower and bed.

She glanced at her watch and quickened her pace. If she got home soon, she'd probably have time to Skype her parents before Mom left for school. The fifteen-hour time difference between Seoul and Minneapolis was sometimes a challenge, but she and her parents had been amazed to discover that communicating with people literally on the other side of the world was as easy as installing a tiny camera on the computer and hitting a few buttons.

Focused on her plans, Claire didn't pay attention to the two men who approached her. Even if she had been more engaged, she wouldn't have perceived them as a threat. Seoul had a reputation as an extremely safe city. Crime, particularly personal crime, was very rare.

Without warning, Claire had a sharp, overwhelming feeling of danger. Only a heartbeat later she felt a hand grab for her. Whether she'd been alerted by a muffled sound, a perception of movement, or simply intuition, Claire suddenly felt compelled to pivot quickly and dive to one side. A man dressed in a dark jacket, his face obscured by a hoodie, lunged after her and arched a fist in her direction. Reflexively, she stumbled backward—narrowly missing the punch—but in doing so, she smacked solidly into the second man. He tried to grab her, but she ducked and flailed in his direction with her elbow. Her blow was partially deflected by his leather coat, but Claire was able to throw off his grasping hands and pull away.

Fueled by an adrenaline rush and pure survival instinct, Claire succeeded in putting a Hyundai SUV between herself and the men. Her heart pounded painfully and she tried to scream, but she knew her anemic shriek couldn't be heard beyond the parking lot. Trying to control her panic, she turned to run back toward the hospital.

Within two steps, however, one of the men grabbed her lab coat, halting her progress. She sensed another blow coming and held up her purse as a shield. Rather than a fist, a knife sliced through the purse and tore into the flesh of her forearm. This time, her scream was much louder, startling her assailants. In that instant, she dropped her purse and staggered back, trying again to flee the attackers. They quickly recovered and followed.

The tenacity her parents had commented on a hundred times saved her life. Although Claire could feel blood dripping from her arm, she turned around and kicked high and hard with her right leg, catching the man with the knife squarely on the chin. He reeled backward, landing hard on the concrete, but the leather-jacketed man lurched toward her and grabbed her injured arm. Claire ignored the pain and with a strength and agility that were completely at odds with her slight frame, she whirled away from the assailant and broke free from his grasp. Once again she started running toward the hospital, screaming for help.

Before she'd covered a hundred feet, she saw two security guards running in her direction. The man with the hoodie shouted and his partner mumbled a reply before he picked something up and ran off with his friend.

Claire's heart was still hammering when the security guards reached her. They noticed her bleeding arm and one produced a handkerchief to help staunch the flow. "Thank you," she said through panting breaths. "Thank you," she whispered a second time and then repeated in Korean, "*Kamsahamnida*."

The guards made no attempt to follow Claire's attackers. Instead, they led her back into the hospital, and took her directly to the Emergency Department. There, the guards turned her over to the staff and called the police.

Within no time, two nurses had cleaned the knife wound and a young doctor was putting a series of neat stitches into the six-inch long gash, all the while telling Claire about completing his plastic surgery residency in Boston. The adrenaline surge was wearing off and the pain in Claire's arm was changing from acutely intense to a merely tear-producing throb. While she was being treated, Claire realized that during the assault she'd lost her purse. On reflection she knew that the man in the leather jacket had picked it up before he fled.

"Well, damn!" she said to no one in particular. Other than about twenty dollars worth of Korean won, she'd just lost her favorite stethoscope, a couple of credit cards and some personal items. And then she remembered…

"Damn!" she repeated. Because Claire's father was a Lutheran minister, she rarely swore. But tonight the circumstances definitely warranted it. She sighed and looked at the doctor who was suturing her fore-arm. "My passport," she said with exas-peration. "They got my passport."

CHAPTER TWO

LIEUTENANT LUKE LLEWELLYN was sitting at a borrowed desk in the security office of the American Embassy in Seoul, reading a recent issue of *Sports Illustrated* and trying to avoid boredom. He was not particularly successful. It was a tedious way to spend a lovely Saturday afternoon, but he really couldn't complain because it beat most of the alternatives.

Luke had been a naval intelligence officer for nearly eight years. He'd completed three tours in the Persian Gulf, where he had logged an inordinate amount of time in the E-2 Hawkeye and other early warning system aircraft, monitoring movements of men and weapons. He'd also spent hours upon hours in front of computer terminals watching satellite feed and listening to interpretations of intercepted conversations, trying to discern plans of the enemy. The work wasn't exactly what he'd signed up for when he applied to the Naval Academy at seventeen, but he had no doubt of the critical, life-and-death nature of his work.

However, with Luke's last promotion, the Navy had "loaned" him to the Army. What followed was the longest nine months of his life. He'd been assigned to a forward operating base in Afghanistan, where his affinity for, and appreciation of, the soldiers and marines who were "boots on the ground" quickly rose in conjunction with his disdain for the Taliban.

While in Afghanistan he decided it was time to consider parting company with the U.S. military, but then he'd been recalled by the Army and sent to South Korea. Compared to the Middle East, life in Korea was a cake walk. There were no snipers, no IEDs and no suicide bombers. The weather was good and the Korean people wanted the military in country—at least for the most part. All in all it was an excellent assignment to close out his career.

As a naval intelligence officer in Seoul, Luke assisted Army personnel in monitoring the communications and activities of the North Korean regime and its allies. That position had him bouncing around the northern part of the country, mostly doing spot reviews across the checkpoints of the demilitarized zone. The DMZ was the military demarcation line between North and South Korea, dating back to the 1950s, when the countries ceased overt conflict. Technically, the war had never ended and both sides continued to heavily arm their respective borders. The DMZ was at least five miles wide and heavily mined, fenced and monitored. Luke also spent significant time at a limited-access area in Seoul's Yongsan Army Garrison. The nondescript building on the north side of the American military installation housed an impressive bank of state-of-the-art computers. Although surveillance work could be tedious, he enjoyed field expeditions with some of the Army guys—riding in Humvees or Blackhawks. And he relished the times when the teams could pass along anomalies or surreptitious movements, alerting the "powers that be" to potential threats or events which might require diplomatic or even military intervention.

In addition to his other responsibilities, Luke was required to take his turn as officer-in-charge of the American Embassy's security detail one weekend each month, even though the Marine guards who were responsible for the embassy needed scant supervision. He was expected to maintain a presence on the embassy grounds, being called on from time-to-time to help manage issues affecting State or Defense Department personnel or problems encountered by any of the thousands of Americans living or visiting the country. Because he wasn't needed all that often, Luke redeemed the time by working out in the embassy's well-equipped gym, watching movies, reading or playing poker with the Marines and consular personnel. One benefit—something he always looked forward to—was the first rate food in the cafeteria.

The slow Saturday afternoon was interrupted by a knock at the open office door, and Marine Staff Sergeant Antonio Mancini entered without waiting for an invitation. Approaching the desk, Mancini waved a file in Luke's direction. "Luke, you lucky dog," he said. "You've got some customers."

Luke remained slouched in his chair. He didn't look up from an article describing the early predictions for the upcoming Major League season. "Customers?" He turned a page. "This is an embassy, Tony, not a department store. We don't have customers."

"Man, oh man," Tony chuckled, and his chocolate-brown eyes crinkled at the corners. "There's a couple of women in the waiting room—real lookers—who need some help."

Luke finally glanced at the sergeant and sighed heavily in feigned exasperation. "Okay, what?"

"Seems one of the ladies' passports was stolen last night along with her purse. She's filed the paperwork to replace it but needs to report being a crime victim. I've taken her statement." He waved the skinny file in Luke's direction again. "Unusual situation… I've been here almost four years, and this is the first time I've seen an American woman knifed by an assailant."

"Seriously?" Luke's nonchalant attitude

evaporated and he threw the magazine on the desk. "She was knifed? How bad?" He sat up straight and took the file.

"Luckily just a flesh wound to her arm."

Luke skimmed the first page and memorized the basics: Mary Claire Olsen…25… Rochester, Minnesota…Registered nurse… Working a month in Korea…Single. "You said there were two. Who's with her?"

"Her roommate—for moral support. The roomie lives here." Tony briefed him on more of the details. "The victim is doing some sort of educational thing at Samsung Medical Center. According to her story, she was attacked by two guys last night right outside the hospital. The second page is the original police report and the third page is the English translation."

"Actually *at* the hospital?" Luke flipped to the third page. "That's in a good part of the city… It's well lit and there are plenty of people around, pretty much twenty-four-seven."

"Yep." The sergeant pointed to the file. "Right there in the police report. The wound was pretty significant. It took a couple dozen stitches to sew her arm up."

"Seriously?" Luke repeated. "Man, this is a first." He closed the folder and stood. "Come on, Tony. Let's go take care of our customers."

AS TONY MANCINI FOLLOWED Luke from the room he was struck for about the twentieth time by the lieutenant's size. He'd known Luke for a year but had known *of* him for nearly a decade. Luke didn't quite rate being called a legend, but he was pretty close. Indeed, it was rare for a man from one of the service academies to be drafted into the NFL, but Luke—an outstanding football player for the Naval Academy—had been selected by one of the pro teams. Tony didn't recall which. In the end, though, Luke had decided to keep his commitment to the Navy and the NFL had lost out.

As he trailed the lieutenant, Tony could certainly see why the NFL wanted him— the man was a *barn*. In his fifteen years in the Corps, Tony had never seen anyone that big wearing a uniform. The man was at least six foot six and weighed somewhere north of 260. Come to think of it,

Tony wasn't certain where Luke got his clothes; he didn't think the Navy made standard uniforms that large.

The embassy's Marine guard detail genuinely liked Luke and enjoyed when he was the weekend officer-in-charge. Luke took the duty seriously—some of the officers didn't—and he didn't look down on the enlisted guys—some of the officers did. Luke was an intelligent and affable Texan, and he'd done several tours in the Middle East—that alone had earned their respect. He was amiable most of the time, but tough when he needed to be. He played a good game of poker and was a magician when anyone was having problems with anything electronic. In addition, he was the only man Tony had ever seen actually bench-press 400 pounds. In truth, the guys were a little in awe of the big man.

AS THE TWO MEN strolled down the wide hallway toward the large waiting area, Tony said, "Heard you were getting out... Any truth to the rumor?"

"Yep." Luke's drawl became more pronounced. "Got three weeks left in Seoul.

I'm off to Honolulu around the first of May to sign papers and get counseled. Then I'm headin' home."

"Well, dang," Tony replied. "Since this is your last weekend with us, we need to pull together a game of Texas Hold 'em. You've got a reputation as an easy mark. We're gonna miss you."

Luke scoffed good-naturedly and opened the door to the large waiting room. He saw two women looking a bit lost among the dozens of chairs.

The American Embassy in Korea was located in a converted seven-story office building. During normal working hours, the waiting area was often standing-room-only.

During the weekends, the embassy was essentially closed, though Americans were allowed in for emergencies. Those situations were evenly split between U.S. citizens experiencing accidents, serious illnesses or even death, and situations in which U.S. citizens—typically young men—got into legal trouble. Most of *those* cases involved too much alcohol. This case was baffling, however, because in nearly a year as substitute duty officer, Luke had never even heard of a case of a random mugging, much less a physical assault on an American woman.

Luke studied the two women as he crossed the wide waiting area. The closer woman was blonde and appeared to be on the tall side. She was attractively dressed in skinny jeans and a snug red sweater. Beyond her was a slender Korean woman, more somberly dressed in a long gray skirt and hip-length tan jacket. Both women stood as the two military men approached and Luke noted that the blonde was indeed—as Tony had remarked—a looker. Her wavy, streaked, shoulder-length hair was brushed back, accenting intelligent blue eyes. Her deep-pink painted lips parted in welcome, revealing pretty white teeth.

Luke had years of training and experience in observation and assimilation of details, and his immediate impression was of a very attractive young woman. But he would have estimated that she was in her mid-thirties, not the 25 that had been reported on the form. Despite her pretty, inviting smile, that vague disconnect piqued his curiosity, causing his naturally skeptical mind to become even more alert.

Shifting his eyes a bit, Luke quickly looked at the Korean woman standing a few paces back. She was a little taller than most of the local women but had the slender build and staunchly erect posture commonly encountered here. Her black hair was pulled up in a clasp and she was wearing dark-rimmed glasses which—along with her rather frumpy clothes—contributed to a "geek chic" look. Luke got the impression that she was more nervous than her friend. She'd appeared ill-at-ease when she saw the uniformed men descending on them. Luke was very aware that his size was disconcerting to most people and was used to the response. Nonetheless, her reaction seemed a little extreme.

Deciding to start with a friendly approach, Luke addressed the tall curvy blonde. He held out his hand, and with his most reassuring smile drawled, "Hello, Ms. Olsen. I'm Lt. Llewellyn. I understand that you had a problem last night. We're here—"

His introduction was simultaneously interrupted by Tony and the blonde.

"Oh, no! Not me—" The blonde's cheeks darkened and she shook her head.

"Uh, Lieutenant—" Tony held up his hand.

Luke glanced back at his comrade who motioned toward the dark-haired woman. "Lieutenant, this is Ms. Olsen." He indicated the blonde who was now grinning. "This is Ms. Jessica Tyson. Ms. Olsen is staying with Ms. Tyson while she's in Seoul."

Luke took a step back and glanced sheepishly between the two women. Trying to smooth over his discomfiture, he shook his head slightly and said, "Uh, sorry. Excuse me." He held out his hand again. "Ms. Tyson, nice to meet you. Sorry for the mix-up."

"Not a problem," she answered, her voice tinged with humor. He shook her hand quickly before turning again to the other young woman, who was still standing several feet away.

She wasn't smiling.

Luke covered the distance in two steps.

This time when he looked at the dark-haired woman he took in details that he'd missed previously. On closer examination he realized that she was not Korean, or at least she was not full-blooded Korean. Her hair, while very dark, was not a flat black. Rather it carried deep brown highlights, and it was very glossy. Her skin was a soft, creamy color rather than the paler shades that many Korean women tried to maintain.

Then Luke realized that the most unusual thing about her appearance—what he should *not* have missed—was her eyes. Now that he was close enough to look past the dark-framed glasses, he could see the color—or rather colors—of her eyes. For the most part they were greenish blue, which alone would have been striking. But what was remarkable was that the outer one-third of both irises was a warm, coppery brown, interrupted periodically by small bluish flecks. The result was stunning.

Luke suddenly realized he'd been staring. Recovering his composure, he held out his hand. "Let me try this again… Ms.

Olsen, I'm Luke Llewellyn, U.S. Navy. I understand that you have an incident to report."

Cautiously, she placed her hand in his and practically gaped. Luke's grip was gentle, but his hand was huge and it completely swallowed her much smaller, finer-boned one. Quickly she pulled her hand back and blinked nervously. "I'm not really sure what I'm supposed to do. Last night the police detective said I would have to come by the embassy to apply for a replacement passport, and that while I was here I should talk to someone about…well about being mugged." Her voice was soft and a little tentative, and she made a slight waving gesture with one hand.

Luke was still recovering from his embarrassment. In his peripheral vision he got a glimpse of Tony trying to keep a straight face. Ignoring his snickering colleague, he gave his best effort to appear competent and reassuring. Using his most professional tone, he explained, "In cases like this, where U.S. citizens are harmed, embassy personnel try to work as closely as possible with the police to resolve the case and ensure that it doesn't happen again. If you'll come with me, I need to get a little more information." He motioned toward the hall that led to his borrowed office.

Claire hesitated a beat before responding, "Yes, okay. But…would it be all right if Jessica comes, too?"

"Of course. Ms. Tyson, you're welcome to accompany us but I'll ask you to avoid interfering."

"Thanks," the blonde replied in a friendly tone. "I promise I'll keep quiet."

Luke led the quartet down the hall with the curvy blonde beside him. Claire Olsen stayed a few paces behind and the Marine sergeant brought up the rear. Trying to appear casual with his initial questioning, Luke asked, "Ms. Tyson, have you been in Seoul very long?"

"It's Dr. Tyson, actually. PhD, not M.D. And yes, I've lived in Seoul about seven years." Her voice was a little throaty, and Luke discerned a bit of a northeastern accent, perhaps New York or another part of New England.

"What do you do?" he asked. They had arrived at the office. Luke entered first and pulled a couple of chairs forward to face the desk. He gestured for the women to sit before retreating behind the desk and taking a seat.

"I'm a professor of cultural anthropology at Seoul National University"

Luke responded, *"Hangukmal hasil jul aseyo?"*

"Yae, jogeumyo. Hangukmal hal jul ani?" she answered, looking amused.

Luke grinned and just shook his head. "No. Other than 'hello', 'thanks,' 'how much' and 'where's the men's room,' that's pretty much the limit of my Korean. Do you actually teach in Korean?"

"No. I teach graduate courses, so my classes are all in English," Jessica replied. "Most of my students want to go to the U.S. to study further, and they need to practice writing and conversing in English."

Luke glanced toward the woman's silent roommate and asked, "How are you two acquainted? Did you know each other before coming to Korea?"

"Seoul National provides me with a very nice three-bedroom apartment," Jessica said. "Although I've lived here for so many years, it can get pretty lonely being a random American in a big city." She shrugged. "From time to time I offer one of my spare bedrooms to visiting scholars."

Luke nodded and turned to Claire. "Is that what you are? A 'visiting scholar'?" He pointed to the form the sergeant had completed. "It says here you're a nurse."

Claire was sitting very erect. Although his question was mild, his tone indicated doubt. She cleared her throat before answering. "Well, kind of." She shifted as if her chair was uncomfortable. "I'm in a graduate program at the University of Minnesota. I'm involved in a project for one of my professors, so I'm working at Samsung Medical Center…collecting data for a research study."

Luke had been jotting notes as she spoke. He glanced up, "What is your professor's name?"

"I'm sorry?" Claire responded.

"The name of your professor in Minnesota…"

"Sung…Dr. Lin-yeong Sung, but she goes by 'Cindy' in the U.S. Dr. Sung is Korean, but she's been working at the Mayo Clinic Hospital for nearly twenty years." Claire seemed to be growing even more uncomfortable. "What does that have to do with me getting mugged?"

"I'm just trying to get background information for the file." He made another note. "What do you do for this 'research study'?"

"I work with children who have cancer."

He glanced back at her and then looked down to scrawl something on his pad. "In what capacity?"

"What difference does that—"

"Please just answer the question." Luke kept his voice without inflection.

"I work on a hematology-oncology unit with children fifteen and under." She squirmed and sighed. "We're collecting data on play therapy involving three different activities—computer games, pets—particularly dogs—and musical instrumentation... We actually teach the children how to play either the piano or a flute. The dependent variable—or rather variables—are symptom experiences and side effects of their therapy—usually a combination of chemo, radiation and sometimes bone marrow transplant."

He didn't respond so she licked her lips then continued. "Specifically, I collect information on when and to what extent the children experience symptoms, including nausea, pain, anorexia, insomnia and depression. I periodically measure salivary cortisol levels and take daily blood samples looking for signs of infection or anemia. We also evaluate other parameters such as anemia, leucopenia, weight gain or loss, vital signs, alopecia and dehydration." Her rapid, matter-of-fact explanation was done in monotone and she stopped abruptly. "Does that answer your question?"

Sometime during her recitation, Luke had stopped writing. He was watching her eyes. Several seconds passed where he tried to come up with a response, but his brain seemed to have clicked off. His mouth was dry and he had to clench his teeth to keep his face expressionless. He knew he was staring and forced himself to look down at what he'd written. Finally, he managed to come up with what he hoped was a reasonable response.

"Hematology-oncology. Is that like leukemia?" He scribbled something.

"Yes, for the most part."

Luke knew it was his turn again. He feigned looking down at the form. "So you've been here a month? How long is your…um…assignment?"

"The fellowship is for three months. I should be here through May."

He jotted something down then sat back in his chair. Staring at her with renewed intensity, he said, "Tell me about last night."

In a few sentences, she told him about being assaulted by two men in the hospital's parking lot. When she concluded, he watched her for a moment. "Ms. Olsen, I'm sure people have told you that physical assaults such as you describe are very rare in Seoul."

"Well, yes… I was told Seoul is very safe. But, evidently not…"

"So, why do you think someone would attack you?"

"Mr., er, Lieutenant…I'm sorry I don't recall your name—"

"Llewellyn," his response was curt, and he motioned toward the name pin above his left chest pocket.

"Lieutenant Llewellyn, I've no idea why someone would attack me. It was dark and I was alone. I guess I looked like an easy target."

"Target for what?"

"I'm sorry?" she said.

"What were you targeted for?"

She blinked several times and sat back in apparent confusion. "Why, my purse, of course. They stole my purse."

"Ms. Olsen, that seems to be the case. But purse thieves don't typically resort to violence. Why do you think you were attacked with a knife?"

"I…I guess it was because I fought back."

"How were you approached? Did they try to grab your purse from the outset?"

She considered his question for a few seconds. "I…er… Now that I think about it, maybe at first they were trying to grab me…"

"Did they say anything?"

She looked pensive. "One kind of yelped

when I kicked at him, but he didn't say anything to me. They might have talked to each other, but I really wasn't attuned to that, and it would have been in Korean...." She blinked and shifted again.

"Why did you fight back? Why didn't you just give them your purse?"

"I don't know. I didn't stop to think about it. It happened really fast. I was frightened and I just...reacted." Each word was spoken with emphasis and mounting irritation. She sat up even straighter and her tone carried a hint of belligerence. "Lieutenant, I don't like being questioned as if I was somehow responsible. All I did was walk across the parking lot. Two men attacked *me!* I lost my purse, some credit cards and my passport. Plus I've got a gash on my arm that's really throbbing right now. I came here to follow up with someone at the embassy. That was what I was told to do, and for some reason you're treating me like it was my fault." Her face was flushed.

This whole case was bothering Luke. He watched her expression through the outburst…she seemed overly defensive, so he persisted with his questions..

"Ms. Olsen, you weigh—what—115? How were you able to fight off two men, at least one of whom had a knife, and come out with only a cut on your arm?"

She lurched from her chair. "That's it. I'm leaving." Her voice was blunt.

Jessica stood, too, and joined the conversation for the first time. "Lieutenant, this type of questioning seems inappropriate—"

Luke remained seated and his expression didn't change. Interrupting both women, he said, "Ms. Olsen, sit down, please."

"I was the victim! I thought someone here was going to help!" Her voice grew louder and her face redder.

Luke stood then, extending to his full height, looming over the two women. He stared into the oddly colored eyes and repeated, "Ms. Olsen, please sit down. You'll need to answer a few more questions." His eyes remained fixed on Claire's although he addressed her roommate. "Ms. Tyson, you can stay or go, it's your choice."

A brief staring match ensued before

Claire exhaled then sat down on the edge of her chair. Jessica glanced at her roommate and copied her.

AS HE WATCHED THE EXCHANGE from his station near the door, Tony was becoming exasperated. He was surprised by Luke's brusque manner and tough interrogation. The lieutenant's scowl was uncharacteristic. He was usually obliging and sympathetic, particularly when working with civilians. Tony's agitation edged toward anger as his superior officer's questions and manner grew increasingly harsh.

Despite Tony's growing consternation, he snapped to attention when Luke addressed him. "Sergeant Mancini, the police report notes that there were surveillance cameras in the parking lot. Have one of the translators contact the precinct office and ask for a detective. See if they can send me a video file or web link so I can review the encounter."

Tony gave an almost indiscernible nod and replied with a crisp "Yes, sir." Immediately, he departed to follow the order.

LUKE CONSIDERED the now-tense women and decided to try to defuse the situation. Addressing Claire but including her friend he said, "Ladies, I'm sorry if my questions seem unsympathetic, but I need to file a complete report." He tried a wry half smile and gave a brief wave to nothing in particular. "You know, the brass and all. They'll have my head if I'm not thorough."

That was actually stretching the truth. He would not be expected to do much beyond cursory data collection, and it was very unlikely that the Marine Duty Officer or any of the consular staff would do more than skim his report on Monday. But something bothered him about the whole episode. Physical crimes of that sort were virtually unheard of—even purse snatchings were rare. Looking at Claire and talking with her, he couldn't conceive of how she could fend off two armed men who were intent on stealing her purse.

But she'd answered his questions about her work without pause—he was certain that part of her account was true. Plus, her roommate had seemed honest—although he would check her story after the women left.

Liars came in all sizes, and gorgeous, arresting eyes aside, the details of the attack didn't make sense. It was conceivable that she'd harmed herself, in some kind of attention-grabbing situation, or maybe she was involved in something sordid or illegal that went wrong. If there was surveillance video, though, he could get a few answers fairly quickly.

"While we're waiting, can I offer you something to drink? We have coffee or all kinds of soft drinks... Water?" His drawl became more pronounced.

Luke's change in manner and engaging grin worked with Jessica. She smiled. "A Diet Coke would be wonderful, if you have one."

"Can do. Ms. Olsen?"

"Just water, please." Her response was flat, and Luke realized the only expressions she'd exhibited so far were frustration, irritation and anger, with maybe a hint of fear or timidity.

"Coming right up." He left the office and quickly proceeded down the hall to the break room. He grabbed a small bottle of water and can of Diet Coke from the refrigerator and quietly jogged back, pausing outside the room hoping to eavesdrop on the women. He was disappointed however, as their voices were pitched softly and he was unable to discern their conversation. He sighed and walked into the room.

"Here, ladies." He gave the can to Dr. Tyson who took it gratefully and popped the top. He handed the water to Claire, who took it from him, carefully avoiding touching his hand. Luke surreptitiously watched as she unscrewed the top and took a quick sip.

"You're right-handed?" It was both a question and observation.

"Yes." Her answer seemed a little hesitant.

"Where is your injury?"

She set her water on the desk and held up her right arm. She pulled back the sleeve of her tan jacket almost to her elbow, revealing a bulky dressing of white gauze encircling her arm. "Do you want me to take off the dressing so you can actually see it?" Her tone was blatantly sarcastic, and her eyes steadily held his.

"I don't think that will be necessary. Can you point to where the wound is?"

She indicated the underside of her forearm, from a few inches under her wrist, nearly to her elbow. Luke felt an odd sense of relief. The placement of the wound supported her story. It suggested a defensive injury, as if she'd held up her arm to ward off the attack. Further, if the cut had been self-inflicted, it was a pretty sure bet her left arm would have been injured. He jotted a note and was about to continue his questions when there was a brief knock at the open door.

"Lieutenant," Tony Mancini didn't enter the room. He caught Luke's eyes and gave a quick nod to his superior officer.

"Excuse me a minute. This shouldn't take long." Luke closed the file, nodded briefly and left the room.

During the short walk to the security office, Tony succinctly filled Luke in. "Getting that footage was a piece of cake. Our translator was able to find a detective—a Mr. Park—who speaks English. While I was still talking to him, that dude emailed me a video link to footage they had already excerpted from the surveillance cameras in the medical center parking lot." He pushed open the door to the security office where two other marines were monitoring the three dozen remote camera screens. They started to rise in deference to Luke's rank, but he nodded to them and they continued working. Tony pointed to a computer at the end of the row. He shook his head and gave Luke a meaningful look. "Wait'll you see this." Both men remained standing while Tony reached down and started the video.

Fortunately the hospital parking lot had been fairly well lit, and the video was of good quality. Luke and Tony were silent as they watched a white-coated Mary Claire Olsen come into view, walking at a brisk pace. She was almost out of the camera's range when a man approached her from behind. At first she jumped out of his way when he tried to grab her, then as he swung his fist, obviously intending to strike her, she seemed to whirl and lean away, barely missing a serious blow. They saw her use her purse as a shield to deflect the arching knife, and then watched as she kicked out and struggled to fend off the two men. Luke swore quietly as she managed to stumble away from the assailants. Although the video was not in color, they could easily discern blood rapidly staining the white sleeve of her lab coat.

There was no audio, but he could tell that she screamed for help and then screamed again. He caught the surprised reaction of the two men as they heard the guards responding to the altercation. Both started to run off, but one paused briefly then ran back to pick up the purse the nurse had dropped. As the men ran out of the camera view, two guards approached from the far side and led the bleeding young woman back to the hospital. According to the time stamps, the entire incident took a little more than ninety seconds.

Luke replayed the video, swore again, and then ran it a third time. He leaned over the keyboard, pulled up his secure email account, and in a few keystrokes quickly saved the link so he could view it again. Finally, he turned to Tony. He looked grim.

"So, what do you think?" the sergeant asked.

Luke stared at the now blank computer screen. "I think I've got to go apologize to our customer," he responded. "Some groveling may be necessary." He paused a breath before adding, "I don't know, but something about that attack still bugs me…" He sighed then and glanced at the sergeant. "What do you think?"

Tony looked at the computer and then back at Luke. He nodded, "Yeah, I think groveling would be appropriate."

CHAPTER THREE

"I'M SURE THEY'RE nearly done." Jessica's tone was hopeful as she tried to encourage Claire. "I can't imagine that he'll have many other questions." She glanced at her watch and grimaced.

Claire looked at her own watch for what seemed like the tenth time in the past hour and sighed. "What time is your date?"

"He's supposed to pick me up at six. I can call him and change it to seven…"

Claire shook her head. "No, that's not necessary, Jessica. You've been terrific through this whole thing. Why don't you go ahead and head home. I can handle it from here, and I won't have a problem finding my way back to the apartment."

Even though they'd known each other for only a few weeks, Jessica had been a stalwart friend. In addition to sharing her home, she had instructed Claire on how to navigate Seoul and she'd taken her to dinner and church on several occasions. Jessica had immediately come to the hospital and supported Claire while she was being stitched up. Then she'd helped translate while Claire had given her statement to the police. Today Jessica had offered to accompany her to the embassy to apply for the replacement passport and report the incident. Claire had quickly accepted her offer because she was still trying to find her way around the huge city.

Initially, the process had been simple. The guards were respectful, allowing them to enter and showing them where to go. The Consular Assistant had filed the paperwork for the replacement passport before directing the women to Sergeant Mancini, who'd been sympathetic and helpful. He'd repeatedly tried to assure both women that Seoul was one of the safest places in the world for single women. He seemed genuinely baffled and angry—ready to beat the daylights out of the perpetrators. After he'd assisted with the intake forms, he described the remaining step in the process—a brief meeting with Security's duty officer. That meeting, he'd assured them, was just perfunctory. They had both been stunned when the alarmingly big officer, with his disarmingly mild drawl, had bombarded Claire with questions and stared at her with distrust.

Claire had not completely recovered her composure following last night's attack. Although trying to seem calm, she was nervous, hesitant and uncharacteristically fretful of strange men. The embassy was large and imposing, but at least she'd been spared the ordeal of being among a crowd of people.

The sergeant had been friendly, but when he returned with his superior officer, she was immediately overwhelmed into a state bordering on panic. Her reaction to the lieutenant was totally out of place—he bore absolutely no resemblance to her attackers, who'd been Korean..

But the lieutenant had alienated her from the outset when he mistook Jessica for her. Since she'd arrived in Seoul, there'd been too many occasions to count in which people assumed she was Korean, but Claire had never been annoyed before. Luke's stereotypical attraction to the pretty, curvy blonde, along with his equally obvious choice to ignore her, bothered her in a way that was unexpected. When he was finally forced to acknowledge her, he was ruthless as he grilled her, and she immediately got the impression that he doubted her account of the attack. She couldn't conceive why he thought she could—or would— make something like that up. Being particularly vulnerable, it bothered her to be questioned and to have someone stare at her as he had, practically accusing her of lying.

"This whole situation is just so weird." Jessica took a sip of her soda. "In all my years here, I've never known anyone who was robbed. And I've certainly never known someone who was attacked—well at least not a woman. I've heard of quite a few bar fights and such…"

She was interrupted when the two uniformed men returned. Claire couldn't tell anything from the sergeant, who was expressionless, but the lieutenant looked vaguely uncomfortable. The big man sat behind the desk while the sergeant remained standing at the door.

Luke leaned forward, placing his forearms on the desk and clasping his hands. Claire once again felt intimidated by his size, but she sensed that his response to her had softened. For the first time she really looked at the man, noting his strong features, high cheekbones and full lips. His close cropped hair was dark blond, contrasting somewhat with dark eyebrows shading hazel eyes. Laugh lines were prominent in their corners, hinting that he smiled a lot.

"Ms. Olsen," he began, his gaze holding hers. She was briefly distracted when she noted the amber striations in his otherwise greenish-brown eyes. "Sergeant Mancini was able to obtain the surveillance footage from last night and we've reviewed it several times." He paused for emphasis. "It confirmed your account of the attack."

"Well, of course—"

Holding up his hand, he interrupted. "But I still have some questions…"

Claire suddenly felt very vulnerable. Her

eyes burned and she blinked several times, trying to keep from falling apart.

Luke abandoned professionalism and reached across the desk to gently pat her hand, surprising them both. Quickly, he pulled back his hand and actually shuffled in his chair.

"I'm sorry, Miss Olsen. Please don't be alarmed." He sounded as if he wasn't used to apologizing. "I need to explain. I'm an analyst. I spend pretty much all day every day trying to understand and interpret information. We're trained to not take anything at face value, and I transferred my ingrained skepticism to your situation. At any rate, my initial mistrust was unwarranted. Please, I sincerely apologize for doubting your account." He glanced at Tony, who responded with a tiny approving nod.

Returning his gaze to Claire he continued, "I needed to get the facts, but I still don't think I have them all." He held up his hand again. "No, not about you, but I'm still trying to put everything together... to get it straight. It simply doesn't make sense."

Claire frowned, but she was willing to accept his explanation and maybe his apology. She swallowed and asked, "What... What else can I tell you?"

He paused to stare at his hands for a moment, evidently contemplating his next question. Finally he met her eyes and asked, "Do you have any martial arts training?"

"Martial arts?" She shook her head. "No. None."

"Are you sure?" His drawl was back.

She gave him a scathing look and huffed, "I thought you'd decided to believe me!"

"You're right. I'm sorry." He sighed. "It's just that the moves you made... On the video... It looked like some sort of kung fu or tae kwon do."

She pressed her lips together and actually smiled for a tiny second. "Uh, no. That was—well—it was from ice skating." Her voice was quiet, nearly a whisper.

"I'm sorry?" It was his turn to look confused. "What about ice skating?"

"The moves."

He still seemed baffled.

"I am—well I used to be—a figure

skater. I guess that last night during the—uh—encounter, the moves just kind of happened." Her voice quieted even more when she said the word "encounter." She paused a breath before continuing. "It wasn't anything I thought about or planned, I just reacted."

Luke sat back in his chair and looked at her with something approaching shock. "Ice skating?" He seemed to reflect on what she'd said, as if replaying the video in his mind. Understanding seemed to dawn. "So that's why you kept going, even after you'd been cut?" It was both a comment and a question.

"Yes, I suppose." She shrugged. "You get used to ignoring pain during training. You fall so frequently that bruises, sprains and even cuts are common, so if you quit every time something hurts, you'd never progress…"

"Well, okay…" He leaned forward in his chair again, staring at his clasped hands. Finally his eyes rose to hold hers. "Miss Olsen. In my experience, I've known a lot of football players and combat soldiers who were easily more than twice your size, who didn't have the fortitude you showed last night." He stood and held his hand as a peace offering. "One of my redeeming qualities is I can admit when I've been wrong. I truly apologize for my harsh questioning and for doubting your veracity. Please let me shake your hand."

Claire was stunned. His eyes pinned hers and she blinked. Nodding slightly, she rose and allowed his huge hand to swallow hers a second time. Marveling at the size difference, she murmured, "It's okay. I understand. You were just doing your job."

LUKE CONTINUED TO STARE at her oddly colored eyes. And then she smiled. The smile was shy and incredibly sweet. The flush that Luke felt was concurrent with an odd tightening in his chest. He recognized the sensation immediately. He had just lost his heart.

CHAPTER FOUR

CLAIRE CRADLED THE little girl in her arms, gently rocking back and forth. She mumbled some words in poorly accented, broken Korean. The child probably couldn't comprehend, but Claire hoped the words would comfort her nonetheless. Hyo-joo was small for her age, having battled leukemia for the past six months. Despite her outward appearance, Hyo-joo was one of the fortunate ones. There were still many hurdles to overcome, not the least of which were opportunistic infections and reoccurrence, but thanks to powerful drugs, radiation and a bone marrow transplant from her father, the child was winning the battle.

They were sitting in the brightly colored playroom of the children's wing. The room was a place of respite—a spot to distract both patients and their families from the pain and uncertainty inherent with cancer—as well as a laboratory. Several years before, a forward-thinking doctor, schooled in both Eastern and Western medicine, had set up the playroom/laboratory to institute a more holistic approach to the management of children with cancer. He'd started with a half dozen electronic play stations with computer games for children from ages one to twenty-one. Those had grown in number, been updated several times, and were perpetually busy from early in the morning until after what should have been the children's bedtime. The computers were a diversion for the very ill children as well as a resource for the doctors and nurses to assess the cognitive and psychomotor function of the young patients. They could also be used as educational tools, as many of the children lost significant time in school when they were hospitalized for weeks and even months.

Claire clucked her tongue and whistled quietly, gaining the attention of the Scottish terrier who'd been resting on a bed in a corner of the large room. "Come,

Kai-ji." The dog jumped up from her perch and happily trotted over to nuzzle the sick girl.

During the second year of the playroom's existence, pet therapy was instituted. The program was started with one small dog; now there were four. In addition to the little Scottie, there was a West Highland white terrier, a cocker spaniel and a standard poodle. The therapy dogs loved children, were patient and well trained, and—very important—they did not shed. Each was remarkably intuitive, somehow knowing which children were ill and limiting rambunctious play with them. Oftentimes the dogs would respond even more appropriately to a child's condition than the nurses and doctors, amazing Claire.

The most recent additions to the holistic therapy program were keyboards and flutes. The hospital had employed a full-time music therapist who taught the children music theory and how to play the instruments. The idea was to help redirect the young patients from focusing on their illnesses to thinking about their recovery. Claire had been skeptical at first, but after working with the therapist and seeing his results, she'd quickly recognized the value of using music to express feelings, particularly for the older children.

WHEN LUKE ENTERED the playroom late Tuesday afternoon, he saw Claire sitting cross-legged on the floor. She was cradling a tiny, bald child who was petting and being licked by a small black dog. He studied the large, brightly lit room filled with computer stations, toys, pianos and keyboards, as well as people whose happy expressions seemed out-of-place for a children's cancer ward.

The children were dressed in loose pajamas that resembled surgeon's scrubs. The younger children's attire was printed with dinosaurs, kittens, horses or princesses and the scrubs of the older children were various solid colors, but were neon-bright. Except that many of the children were holding onto or sitting right beside IV poles and/or were wearing masks covering their mouths and noses, he could have been in a school or children's play area anywhere. All of the adults were either playing with the children or sitting quietly by and reading or watching TV.

When Luke saw Claire, she was engrossed with the child. As he watched, she gently kissed the bald head, smiled and whispered something. The sensation Luke experienced at that moment was completely unique for him. Even during his most vulnerable circumstances, whether he'd been playing football against a tough opponent, or facing tense situations on the war's frontline, or riding in a plane landing on an aircraft carrier in rough seas, he'd never felt this particular combination of apprehension and anticipation. His palms were sweaty, his mouth was dry and his heart beat erratically.

Luke spent much of his life trying to avoid being conspicuous. He'd learned to stand very still to keep from attracting attention. Normally he had at least some success, but in a room filled with about a dozen Korean children and at least that many smallish, slender, black-headed men and women, the huge American man in jeans and green polo shirt was impossible to miss. Before he'd even gotten completely through the door, one of the children squeaked something and within seconds all heads—including Claire's—had turned in his direction. Even the dogs seemed to be aware of his presence.

With a room full of staring men, women and ill children, Luke did his best to appear non-threatening. He gave a small, friendly wave to no one in particular and graced the room's inhabitants with a shy smile. He tucked his hands into his jeans pockets and slumped, trying to shrink.

Claire was startled by his sudden appearance. Still holding the child, she stood gracefully.   "Uh…em…Lieutenant…" When she spoke, all eyes moved from the huge man at the door to her. She cleared her throat and managed to mutter, "Do you need something?"

He nodded. "Yes. I'd like to speak to you for a minute."

Claire passed the little girl to one of the nursing assistants standing nearby. She brushed a hand over her hair and adjusted her glasses before crossing to the door. Once there, she seemed nearly overwhelmed. She blinked tensely as she looked up at him.

"Is there a problem with my case?"

He glanced beyond her into the room full of curious faces and then back down at the anxious young woman. "Is there somewhere quiet we can talk?"

Claire took one step to the side, as if afraid to turn her back on him. She motioned down the short hall leading to a large waiting room in the outer lobby.

"Yes. I'm sure we can find a spot this way." She glanced at him as she led him toward several unoccupied chairs at one corner of the lobby. "Um, why are you here? Is something wrong?"

Luke studied her for a moment before responding. "Has anyone from the consular staff contacted you?"

He was struck again by her unusual eyes and fine, soft features. She was tall and slender, and she was dressed much as she had been on Saturday, in a long dark skirt made of some knit material that flowed. Her pale pink blouse was mostly covered by the buttoned white lab coat and she was wearing soft-soled, flat ballet slippers.

She was remarkably lovely, but there was something extra, something elusive about her that drew him.

Under the cuff of her right sleeve he noted the edge of the gauze dressing and cringed inwardly, envisioning a knife tearing through her soft skin. His mouth tightened as he realized anew how much worse the attack could have been.

"About my passport? I thought they said it could take up to two weeks."

"No. I don't have anything to do with that." They had reached the chairs and he motioned for her to take a seat. She settled obediently, but remained sitting very straight and on the edge, as if she could be ready to bolt if the need arose. Luke scooted another chair around to sit facing her. "No one called you back to follow up on the attack?" His tone betrayed his annoyance, bordering on anger. She shook her head and he took a deep breath and frowned. "I left a detailed report which instructed the attaché to order one of the embassy personnel to let you know what I learned about the assault."

Claire sat up even straighter. "Lieutenant…um…Llewellyn… No. No one has called…"

He sighed and slumped back in his chair a bit. "Look, first, please call me Luke. I'm not here in any official capacity. That…" He motioned randomly with one hand. "Working at the embassy isn't my real job. I'm just a weekend substitute. They—the embassy personnel—were supposed to let you know…" He paused, frowning again.

"Know what?"

Luke leaned forward, ensuring he had her full attention. "I spent the better part of Sunday reviewing all of the hospital's surveillance feed." One corner of his mouth turned up in a half grin. "By the way, they're very well covered—in regard to monitoring what goes on—particularly the doors and the parking lots." He pointed to a camera mounted near the ceiling about twenty feet away from where they sat. The grin faded and he said, "At any rate, I had to go back several hours from the time of the attack, but I was finally able to spot the two assailants. I figured out when they got to the hospital and pieced together what they did while they were here."

She was watching his expressions with mingled curiosity and concern. "Okay. That sounds like a good idea... But why?"

"I told you, the attack bothered me. It didn't make sense and still doesn't." His lips tightened and he looked uncomfortable. "Anyway, I had to go back nearly six hours to find when the two men arrived. They came here at about five, long before they attacked you." He frowned at her and asked, "What time do you normally leave?"

"It varies. Sometimes as early as five or six, but sometimes much later." She shrugged. "Last Friday was one of the later times." She looked perplexed. "I'm not sure where you're going with this."

Luke fought the urge to reach over and rub her hand or pat her cheek—anything, just to touch her. Instead he shoved his hands into his pockets. "Miss Olsen... Can I call you Mary?"

She blinked a couple of times before answering. "No...um... Yes, of course. But I go by Claire. My parents call me 'Mary Claire,' but to everyone else, I'm just 'Claire'."

He smiled then. It was his first genuine smile since he'd walked into the playroom and tried to put its occupants at ease. Claire's breath caught. Her own face softened and her lips turned up slightly in response.

"Okay, just Claire it is…" He sat back up at attention and the smile died away. "Claire," he repeated, "the bottom line is this: the attack wasn't random. They were waiting on *you*. They'd been watching *you* for *at least* five hours and followed *you* into the parking lot."

Disbelief clouded her expression. "How can you know that?" She shook her head and waved her hand dismissively. "Likely they were just waiting for a lone woman, someone who looked vulnerable."

He shook his head. "No. There's no doubt. Claire, this *is* what I do. Like I told you, I only act as babysitter to a bunch of Marine guards occasionally. What I've spent much of the past six years doing is reviewing and interpreting surveillance video."

He glanced around to ensure that there was no one in the vicinity and continued quietly, "Claire, during the time between when they arrived and when they followed you out, at least fifty women exited the building alone. They weren't looking for a vulnerable woman to mug... They were waiting for you." She paled a little then. He gritted his teeth and looked down at the polished floor before allowing his gaze to capture hers again. He was weighing how to proceed. "And something else," he said, leaning a little closer. "I'm pretty sure they weren't intending to steal your purse." His voice quieted to almost a whisper. "Claire, I think they may have been trying to harm you, maybe even kill you."

She surged to her feet and paced several steps away before whirling around to face him again. Her voice was quiet but emphatic. "That's impossible! I don't know anyone in Seoul." She struggled to keep her voice calm as she took a few steps back toward him. "I've only been here a few weeks, for goodness' sake. I'm just a nurse from Minnesota. I haven't done anything wrong and haven't harmed anyone. I don't have anything anyone would want!" She moved away again and then sighed. "Look, you've made some sort of error."

Luke remained seated, still trying to keep a low profile. "I'm sorry, Claire. There is no mistake." He pinched the bridge of his nose in fatigue and frustration. "I left a detailed report for the consular attaché on Sunday. I strongly suggested that someone contact you to tell you what I found and warn you to be wary. It's clear that request wasn't heeded." He sighed and swore under his breath. "I've been—um—away since Sunday night. I just returned from a recon detail this morning and came by to check on you. I hoped you'd been told to be alert and take precautions."

"Lieutenant—"

"Luke," he interrupted. "Like I said, I'm not here officially."

"Okay." She bit her lip then started over. "Luke, I really appreciate your concern. You've gone above and beyond." She smiled slightly. "But there's no reason someone—anyone—would want to hurt me." She paused a breath then sat back down, shaking her head. "The only explanation I can think of is that I was mistaken for someone. Do you think that's possible?"

"Maybe, but I'm doubtful. They were here, waiting for you." He sighed again. "Look, please at least consider the possibility. Don't go anywhere alone and pay attention to your surroundings. And if *anything* even remotely suspicious happens, contact the hospital security guards or the police *and* the embassy." The last sentence was spoken authoritatively, as if he was giving an order.

"Yes, sir." She gave him a small smile. "I will, sir."

His own lips turned up slightly, but he still looked frustrated. There seemed to be nothing left to say. The interview was over. They both stood and Claire held out her hand. "Thank you very much for coming all the way here to talk to me, Luke. It was very considerate of you."

He looked down at their clasped hands. Hers was slender, delicate and soft; his was large, thick and imposing. Despite the contrast, he sensed the unexpected strength that had helped her fight off two men in a dark parking lot.

"Not a problem." He grinned again and said, "I could've lied and said I was in the neighborhood and decided to stop by, but I thought you'd see past that one."

She chuckled and pulled back her hand. "Well, the medical center is a bit away from the Army base..."

They started toward the hospital's entrance. She intended to walk him out, but before they had covered much ground, he placed a hand on her arm, stopping her. "Um, Claire. One more thing."

She turned to face him and her eyes climbed hesitantly up the considerable distance to meet his. She swallowed and said, "Yes?"

"Will you have dinner with me?"

Claire took a half step back and bit her lip. Luke could tell that her mind was racing, hastily trying to come up with an excuse—any reason she could use to plausibly but politely decline his invitation. He cringed inwardly. He *really* didn't want to beg, but he was willing to do whatever it took. Claire's lips parted and he knew she was going to say "no," so he forestalled her. Very quietly, he added one word. "Please."

IT WAS THE "PLEASE" that did it, Claire mused later. Well, that and the random, funny and sometimes oddly sweet smiles that contrasted so markedly with his imposing presence. It was also his intensity and the concern he'd displayed by coming to see her, despite being almost dead on his feet. It was his sharp, knowing hazel eyes with the amber flecks, and it was his impossibly large hands; hands that could obviously be deadly, given their size and strength, but hands that felt gentle, strong and protective when holding hers.

Claire took a shallow breath. She couldn't hide her apprehension as she searched his eyes. Her nod was very slight, and she said, "I need to go report to the charge nurses and finish charting. That shouldn't take more than twenty or thirty minutes. Do you mind waiting?"

The smile that crossed his face dispelled any lingering doubts. He gestured toward the playroom with his head. "I saw the latest iteration of Super Mario on one of the computers. You think I can interest one of the kids in a game?"

Claire's smile mirrored his. "Yes, I'm

certain you can. But I've got to warn you,
they'll beat the daylights out of you. Those
kids are brutal!"

CHAPTER FIVE

THIRTY MINUTES LATER, Claire returned to
the playroom. After reporting to her colleagues and completing her charting, she'd
slipped into the nurses' lounge where she
quickly brushed her hair. For a moment,
she thought about leaving it down, but she
coiled her hair back into a knot and secured it with a large clip. She dabbed on
lip gloss and rinsed her sweaty palms. Her
last act before rejoining Luke was making
a quick call to Jessica.

"Um, hey," she said when her roommate
answered. "I just wanted to let you know
I'm going to be home late this evening."
She took a breath. "I have a date."

"Fun!" Jessica replied. "Who's the lucky
guy? That cute doc who did his residency
at Johns Hopkins?"

"Uh, no. It's the lieutenant from Saturday—Luke."

"What?" Jessica barely stifled a shriek. "Oh my *gosh!* How in the world did *that* happen?"

"He came by the hospital this evening to talk to me. It kind of took me by surprise, but, well, he seems nice, don't you think?"

"I don't know about nice, but he gives new meaning to the term 'hunk.'" Claire heard her friend chuckle. "Now that I think about it, he did seem to be taken with you... *Oh my gosh!*" she repeated.

Claire glanced at her watch. "Look, I've got to go. I'll fill you in when I get to the apartment."

"Okay, but keep your phone with you all the time, and try to call and let me know how it's going. Not that I don't trust the lieutenant, but I want to make sure you're safe and all."

"Yes, Mother." Claire smiled into the phone. "I'll be careful."

Clicking off, she glanced in the mirror again and noted that her cheeks were flushed. That wasn't surprising—her heart rate must be well above a hundred. She grabbed her new purse and lightweight jacket from her locker and took a deep breath. "Well, here goes," she murmured.

THIS TIME THEIR roles were reversed. Claire stood at the door and watched in astonishment as the very large American man sat cross-legged on the floor surrounded by six Korean children and several adults. He was engaged in a heated video game match, and from all appearances, she concluded that he was getting soundly defeated by a twelve-year-old boy named Heen-nak.

Exaggerated groans and growls from Luke mingled with giggles, cheers and jeers from the children. Finally, Luke tossed down his control box. He clutched his chest and fell to one side moaning, "You got me… That's it… I surrender!"

Several children, a couple clutching IV poles, mobbed him. After a few moments, Luke sat up and fist-bumped the young victor. "Great game, dude!" He glanced at one of the adults, who translated. The boy smiled shyly. Luke gently patted the boy's head and glanced toward the door. Spying Claire, he stood. "Thanks again, partner.

I've got to go now, but I'll practice up some and maybe we can have a rematch soon."

He waited for the translator and the young boy grinned and nodded his head. "Thank you, mister."

All eyes were on the huge man as he strode across the room. Claire saw appreciation in Luke's face as he moved toward her, and her heart rate intensified. No man had ever looked at her that way before, with admiration tempered by respect.

"Are you ready to go?" The corners of his eyes crinkled as he smiled at her.

Her own smile was shy and a little uncertain. "Yes, I'm all checked out and charted."

Luke walked very close to Claire as they crossed the lobby. It was nearing dinner time and the hospital was teeming with patients, family members and hospital staff.

Luke was both more and less imposing than before. Wearing his uniform, he'd been disconcerting, simply because the clothing conveyed such authority. The loose-fitting uniform shirt, however, had camouflaged his daunting size. Although Luke's polo shirt was not tight, Claire couldn't help but notice the bulk of the heavy muscles in his chest and arms and the thickness of his neck.

Luke's size probably attracted attention back in the States, so in Korea, he was nothing short of a giant. As a result, his efforts to study the crowd—trying to spot anyone who seemed unduly interested in Claire—were hampered by the fact that pretty much everyone was staring at him. He didn't seem too concerned, however. Perhaps because any potential assailants would be forestalled by his presence.

Initially both Luke and Claire were a little stilted. Luke tried to break the ice as they exited the building. "Thanks for coming with me like this. I know it's short notice and all…"

Claire peered up at him and realized that he seemed to feel as self-conscious as she did. That such a self-assured man seemed nervous helped dispel some of her own anxiety. "Thanks for asking." She smiled then glanced away. "I haven't gotten out much since I've been in Seoul. It'll be fun to go somewhere other than Jessica's apartment and the medical center."

The early awkwardness was starting to crack and Luke seemed more at ease. "Really? So, you haven't had a chance to see much of Seoul?"

"No. I've worked nearly every day since I've been here. On Sundays I've gone to church with Jessica, but it's a little daunting because she attends a Korean church and almost all of her friends and colleagues are Korean."

He seemed to take her disclosure as a challenge. "Well, let's see what we can do about that."

Claire had to tamp down a twinge of fear as they entered the parking lot. Luke noticed her scouring the area. He didn't comment, but lightly placed his hand on her arm. He led her to a nondescript beige Kia sedan and opened the passenger door, ushering her in. She couldn't help a slight giggle as she saw him folding into the driver's side a moment later. "Is this your car?"

"No, thankfully," he said wryly. "It's part of Yongsan's non-official fleet. Base personnel can check out a car on a first-come-first-served basis. Believe it or not, this is one of the larger vehicles." He grinned at her. "The only cars I fit comfortably in are full-size pickups and SUVs—not these mini things. Of necessity I've learned to manage." He started the engine. "Any preference on what you'd like for dinner?"

She smiled at him, realizing that sometime in the past few minutes, she'd lost her nervous edginess. "Actually anything that isn't kimchi and doesn't smell like fish sounds great… In other words, I'd love something remotely American."

He grinned again. "Pizza?"

"Perfect."

"I know just the place. There's an Italian restaurant on Itaewon that does a terrific Chicago–style pizza." He put the Kia into drive and headed toward the exit.

"I've not yet been to Itaewon," Claire said.

Luke chuckled. "Well, there's a first time for all of us. I'm sure you've heard about it. It's kind of a cross between 5th Avenue in New York City and New Orleans's Bourbon Street. Plus, it's only a couple of miles from the Yongsan Army Base, so there are a lot of servicemen and a number of…not particularly reputable people." He looked a little sheepish. "Well, you'll see."

Fifteen minutes later, Luke pulled into a parking spot in a very busy commercial area and Claire was able to take in the street first hand. She saw bustling department stores interspersed with classy restaurants and dives. Coffee shops were adjacent to small stores selling everything from T-shirts to leather goods to gold jewelry to knock-off purses and shoes. Street vendors sold CDs, DVDs and cigarettes, as well as an assortment of food items—most of which Claire didn't recognize and didn't find particularly appealing.

During the three-block walk to the Italian restaurant, Luke kept Claire closely at his side, with his hand on the small of her back. Instinctively, she leaned slightly toward him, enjoying the sensation of protection. He didn't stand out nearly as much here, as at least one-third of the crowd were Westerners. Many of the men and women were obviously military, although only a few were in uniform.

The restaurant they entered could have been located in any city in the U.S. Although it was crowded at the dinner hour, they were quickly ushered into a booth. Settled into her spot, Claire studied her surroundings. The tables were covered in white cloths and graced with small vases of flowers and votive candles. The aroma of garlic, basil and tomatoes permeated the room. The patrons were a decided mix of locals and visitors, mostly dining in pairs and small groups. A waiter handed them each a menu and in passable English asked for drink orders.

"Would you like some wine?" Luke asked.

"No, thanks. I don't drink much, but go ahead if you wish."

"Can't tonight. I'm actually 'on call.'" Luke requested a soda from the waiter.

"I'll have the same," Claire said, and the server nodded, saying he'd be back shortly for their order.

"On call for what?" Claire asked. "Is it for the embassy?"

"No, it's for my day job. Actually, day, night, whenever job. I don't exactly keep regular hours. The embassy gig is necessary because I'm Navy and they don't have enough Marine officers here to do weekend duty—long story—anyway, I'm glad now to have done it because that's how I met you." His quick smile was genuine, and Claire felt an odd flutter in her stomach. She blushed and glanced down to her menu.

"So, tell me about your 'whenever job.'"

He shrugged. "I review surveillance feeds all day and write reports to send up the chain of command. Sometimes I go into the field to verify impressions…pretty routine stuff…"

Claire doubted that anything he did was routine, but he seemed hesitant to go deeper. "How long have you been here doing surveillance?"

"About a year. Before that, I was stationed in several places—mostly the Persian Gulf and the Middle East." He'd been studying her face and abruptly changed the subject. "You have the most unusual eyes I've ever seen." His voice was quiet, with a pensive quality, almost as if he'd spoken his thoughts out loud.

Claire glanced down at her napkin and then back up to catch his gaze. "Yes, uh…"

She shifted awkwardly and pressed her lips together. "It's called 'sectoral heterochromia iridis' if you want the technical name. Basically, it's just an irregular pigmentation of the iris." She took a breath. "I've had to respond to questions about it all my life…"

He looked sympathetic but didn't drop the subject. "So you get a lot of people staring when they notice?" It was both question and comment. "I get the same reaction when anyone sees my feet."

His offhand comment startled a giggle from Claire, and she couldn't prevent a side glance to the floor to study his shoes. He hadn't been joking. Luke's eyes crinkled at the corners at her raised eyebrows.

In seconds, she grew serious again. "When I was a kid it really bothered me when people said something about my eyes. I hated being different from the other kids, and I was really shy." She looked up again; his gaze had not faltered. "Anyway, when I was old enough I made my parents get me colored contacts, so my eyes would just be brown. That helped a lot, but…" She sighed deeply. "Well, I was so happy with the contacts that I stupidly wore them all the time. After about a year, I ended up with pretty severe corneal ulcerations, and came close to needing a cornea transplant. That was the end of the contacts and so…" She gave him a small frown and motioned to her glasses.

He shook his head and murmured, "Kids can be dumb… I think they're beautiful."

The room suddenly seemed to be closing in and Claire felt a little dizzy. That feeling was accompanied by a lightness in her chest and tears threatened. She blinked self-consciously and returned her gaze to her napkin. Her heart rate soared and her stomach quivered. He couldn't know that with that simple statement—with those four words—Luke had helped salve a wound that was more than twenty years old. In that brief moment, years of distress and embarrassment over her unusual eyes were replaced by a sense of release edging into quiet exultation.

He had called them beautiful.

Claire's attention was brought back to the moment when the waiter placed cool glasses of Coke in front of them. "What you want to eat?" he asked.

Luke shifted his gaze to the waiter and said, "Sorry, we're not ready. Can you give us a minute?"

"Of course. I will return shortly." He moved on to the adjacent booth.

Slightly dazed, Claire took a sip to quench her suddenly dry mouth. Setting the glass down, she picked up her menu and tried to focus. She was not entirely successful.

"Their pizza is terrific, but they do great lasagna and pasta, too."

Claire was still reeling from the emotional onslaught brought on by his comment, but she managed to say, "I've had my heart set on pizza since you mentioned it. I'm partial to pepperoni but hate anchovies. Otherwise, I like pretty much anything."

"Got it. Note to self, in the future, don't order pizza with anchovies."

Claire smiled then, recognizing the implications of his comment. As Luke turned to get the attention of the waiter, his cell phone rang. He glanced at her and said something under his breath before pulling the device from his pocket. After scanning the caller ID, he pushed a button on the phone and growled, "Llewellyn."

Although there was little overt change in Luke's expression, she saw a muscle flex in his jaw. "How long ago?" He nodded absently at the response and looked pensive. "How many?…Have you notified ROK command?…Okay, contact them to be on alert status." He looked at his watch. "I'll be there in about fifteen." Luke ended the call and then glared at Claire. Shaking his head, he sighed deeply.

"What's wrong?"

"I've gotta go." His scowl was almost comical. "Maybe I'm being punished for being mean to my brothers or not cleaning my room or something…" He got the attention of the waiter. "We have to leave. Please give me the check."

The waiter nodded and said, "One minute." He departed toward the kitchen.

"Anything serious?" Claire asked.

"No, not really. Looks like there's a squid boat in the Japan Sea with too many people."

She blinked. "Why does the U.S. Army care how many people are on a squid boat? Are they afraid the boat will sink?"

He chuckled. "Uh, no. But a larger-than-normal contingent of men could be a potential threat to the mainland. Most likely, though, they're North Korean refugees."

She nodded, her curiosity piqued. "But it's night. How do you know how many people are on a random fishing boat somewhere out at sea?"

Luke gave her an enigmatic look but didn't answer.

"Oh…I get it. If you told me, you'd have to kill me?"

He chuckled. "Nothing *that* dire. But I'm *not* going to tell you."

She giggled and then became more serious. "What happens if they are refugees?"

His smile faded. "There are surprisingly few people who actually escape from the north. No one can get through the DMZ because of the mines and heavy fortification. A few hundred per year come through China, but the Chinese government really discourages that and will send them back if they're caught—and it's very bad for those who are sent back. Fewer people come by boat, mostly because they lack the resources and opportunity. At any rate, the ROK—Republic of Korea—never turns them away. There are lots of agencies here to help refugees assimilate…"

He was interrupted when the waiter gave him the check. Luke glanced at it then pulled several bills from his wallet and handed them to the waiter. "Thanks. We'll try again tomorrow." He rose and waited for Claire, then stood to one side, indicating that she should precede him.

"You know," Claire said as they left the restaurant, "I've heard that when some people go on blind dates, they'll have a friend call them an hour into the evening with an 'emergency,' to give them a way out…" She winked at him.

Luke scoffed. "Believe me, honey, this is *not* one of those times." He looked relieved that she was actually joking with him. "Can we…um… Would you consider trying again tomorrow?" His eyes were practically pleading.

She smiled. "Yes, of course. But if you

get another mysterious phone call before I get pizza, I'll be very suspicious!"

"I promise. If you'll come with me again, no phone calls!"

As they approached the Kia, he glanced at Claire. "What kind of identification do you have with you?"

"Huh?"

"Do you happen to have your temporary passport?"

"Well, yes." She touched her purse. "Why?"

"What about a driver's license or some kind of picture ID?"

"I have my hospital ID but not a driver's license since I don't drive here... Why?" she repeated.

"Good. That'll make it easier."

"Make what easier?" Claire was getting increasingly confused.

"Getting you on base. I have to get back *now*, so I can't drive you home."

"Why do I need to go onto the base?" She motioned to the very busy street. "It's not a problem. I can just catch a taxi."

"No." His tone was blunt. "That's not an option."

"Wait a minute! Of course it's an option." She stopped walking and turned to face him. "Seriously, Luke, I understand that you need to get back to the base right now, but you don't need to worry about me. I can take care of myself." Her tone suggested it would be wise if he didn't argue.

"Mary Claire—" his drawl was back, much stronger than before "—in case you've forgotten, the reason I came to see you today—well, at least part of the reason—is because I'm convinced someone targeted you the other night. Someone who fully intended to hurt you. *I* can't take you home, but I *can* make sure you get home safely, which is why I need to get you on base." He took her hand and started again in the direction of the car.

She had already lost the battle, softening even further when he'd called her "Mary Claire." Besides, she *really* liked the feel of his large hand enclosing hers. Trying to accommodate to his need to hurry, she said, "Luke, you're sweet for worrying about me, but this is only tonight. You can't be with me tomorrow morning when I go to work or tomorrow evening, or the next day, or the next." She glanced at him and the corners of her mouth turned up a little, "Well…tomorrow evening…" she said hopefully.

"I know," he said, his expression somber. "But I can be sure tonight. I promise that you're going to be safe tonight." There was a hint of something ominous in his tone. "This is my watch, Claire. Nothing is going to happen to you on my watch."

PER LUKE'S INSTRUCTION, Claire's escort not only walked her to the door, but he waited until Jessica answered and questioned her as to whether everything was in order before he left. Following Korean customs, Claire slipped off her shoes and placed them on a small rack in the entry.

Jessica practically pounced on Claire as she closed and locked the door. "Okay, who was that and why are you home already? And where is Lieutenant Luke?"

"That was Mr. Kim. He's one of the local men who work on the Army base. He helps with translation and transportation—that sort of thing. Anyway, Luke was called in to take care of an emergency and he pretty much conscripted Mr. Kim to bring me home.

"What happened?" Jessica persisted.

"Let's go to the kitchen," she replied. "Dinner was interrupted, and I'm starved."

In the small kitchen, Claire pulled some crackers and peanut butter out of the pantry, grabbed a plate and sat down at the table with her friend. Between bites, she ran though the events of the evening, explaining how Luke had stopped by the hospital, ostensibly to warn her of a possible threat but also to ask her to dinner. She grinned when she recounted his shy hesitance. Claire described their walk down Itaewon to the Italian restaurant and how he'd been called just as they were about to order pizza. "When he drove us onto the base, the guard waited with me at the car while Luke disappeared into one of the buildings and came back with Mr. Kim."

"And then…." Jessica prompted.

"And then, what?"

"So Luke just waved goodbye and walked away with a 'see you later, baby'?"

"Not exactly." Claire grinned.

"Well, what exactly? I want details."

"He was very gentlemanly." Claire smiled as she took a bite of a peanut butter covered cracker. "He took my hand and asked what time I wanted to try dinner again."

Jessica snatched a cracker. "And then?"

"Okay, he kissed me." She blushed. "It was very sweet…"

In truth, it *was* sweet—and romantic as all get out. She replayed the memory a few hours later when she was trying to go to sleep. She recalled standing beside the Kia with Luke obviously frustrated by having to leave her. The base was very well lit, but he'd pulled her aside to a spot where they stood in shadow, away from nosy passersby. He'd taken her hand lightly in his. "Is it okay if I stop by about six tomorrow?"

"Yes, please. Six will be perfect."

The cool breeze blew a strand of her hair onto her glasses. Luke gently moved the lock back, then leaned down to lightly touch his lips to her forehead. He regained his full height and brought her hand to his lips. With a brief smile he'd said, "See you tomorrow, Mary Claire. Please, take care."

Then he gazed at her a second longer before he turned and jogged to the adjacent building.

She was smiling sometime later when she finally went to sleep.

CHAPTER SIX

CLAIRE FINISHED CHARTING her patients' progress by five the following evening. She had dressed more carefully than usual that morning and was wearing neat black slacks and a sweater her mother had bought her the previous Christmas. She'd never worn it because the turquoise cashmere actually accented the unusual coloring of her eyes, something she'd always avoided.

Feeling a bit giddy, Claire took a few minutes to freshen her lip gloss and comb her hair. After a moment's contemplation, she decided to leave her hair down and it fell in glossy waves well past her shoulders. Even with her glasses, she was pleased with her reflection. She took a deep breath before heading to the playroom.

In a virtual replay of the previous evening, Luke was sitting cross-legged on the floor surrounded by a set of scrub-clad kids. He was playing Angry Birds with an adolescent boy wearing a mask. Giggles, shouts, cheers and a little grumbling were heard from the group, and a couple of the children were actually trying to help Luke, giving him pointers and instructions using pantomime, broken English and rapid Korean.

Luke saw Claire enter and acknowledged her with a quick wave and a broad wink before returning his attention to the screen. "One more...one more...one more... Oh man..."

He sighed and threw up his hands in defeat. "You got me again." His tone was comically downcast. "Thanks, partner. *Kamsahamnida*," he said with a smile. The beaming boy was being congratulated by his fellow patients, as well. Luke patted his shoulder and then gave the child a slight bow.

He nodded a farewell to the small crowd of parents, hospital personnel and kids as he rose to join Claire. His gaze swept over her, missing nothing, then returned to meet her eyes.

"You've been sandbagging," he mumbled.

Claire was gratified by his stunned look but a little confused by the comment. "I'm sorry?"

He continued to stare. Pointing to her hair, he said, "You've been hiding behind long skirts, glasses and pulling your hair up. You look amazing."

"Thank you." Claire blushed. Pleased, but self-conscious from his compliments, she glanced at her watch, trying to change the subject. "I'm sorry, I thought you said six o'clock. Have you been here long?"

"I got here a little before five. Let's just say I was anxious. Besides, I wanted a rematch. I had this idea that I would vindicate myself from the shellacking I took yesterday." He sighed dramatically. "That didn't happen. I got soundly trounced—again."

She laughed appreciatively. "Thanks for playing with the kids. They loved it. And anything we can do to help them mentally and emotionally promotes their recovery."

Luke frowned a little and his voice quieted. "Um, that boy I was playing with—I think he said his name was Min-soo. Is he going to be all right?"

Claire gave him a quick nod. "Yes. The oncologist thinks he's in remission now. He'll probably go home in a week or so if his blood counts continue to improve. And thanks again for your attention. It seems like a little thing, but it was big to him."

Luke looked relived and then took her hand as they headed to the parking lot.

As they had the previous evening, Claire and Luke made their way down busy Itaewon Street and into the Italian restaurant. A different waiter seated them and took their drink orders.

"Are you going to get another mysterious call in the next thirty minutes?" she teased.

"Gosh, I hope not." He gave her a wry look. "I'm still more or less on call, but I've threatened the duty NCO with dire ramifications if we're bothered." She grinned at his vehemence.

The NCO complied and they talked—interruption free—almost non-stop as they dined on pizza and soft drinks, followed by a shared slice of cheesecake.

"I found some videos of you skating on-line," Luke said between bites. "You were great."

Claire shrugged. "Thanks. I was all right, but I couldn't quite break into the top ten in the national standings."

"I saw footage from a competition in San Francisco about ten years ago—you were what, about fifteen? You were ter-rific."

"That was a pretty good meet. I finished seventh—one of my best. It would have been better if I'd landed my triple." She gave him a self-deprecating smile.

"So, why did you quit?"

"Several reasons, actually. Into the next year—when I was sixteen—I injured my left knee. Not a full ACL tear, but I had to have arthroscopic surgery and was out most of the season. About the same time, my mom was diagnosed with breast can-cer. Skating is very expensive. World-class skaters can get sponsors, but for me, it was all on my parents. When Mom got sick, I didn't want to be a burden financially. So, I quit to help take care of her.

"How's she doing now?"

"Oh, fine!" Claire beamed. "She had surgery and radiation and thankfully, there's been no recurrence for more than eight years."

"But you never went back to skating?"

"No, but that was okay. I had probably peaked, anyway. I was a really good spinner, but only average at jumping." Luke looked as if he wanted debate the point, but Claire continued. "That's when I got interested in nursing—specifically oncology nursing. Helping take care of Mom gave me a feeling that I can't really explain—it was kind of like a 'calling.' I believe—no, I know—that it's important." She blushed a little, surprised by her own passion.

"Anyway, because of the skating, I had been home-schooled in my later years and was pretty much done with high school, so I decided to start college. I graduated when I was twenty and started grad school."

Luke already knew much of what Claire told him. He'd actually spent hours on the internet searching for every scrap of information he could find. Luke had told himself he wanted to figure out why someone would want to harm her. But the truth was, he was infatuated.

With his abilities and resources, he'd been able to learn where she grew up and that she was an only child. He knew that her father was a pastor of a large Lutheran church and her mother had been a teacher before retiring to support her daughter's skating.

Claire had stopped skating and started college at sixteen and gone on to earn her bachelor's degree from the University of Minnesota. He knew that she'd worked in the pediatric oncology unit of the Mayo Hospital before going to graduate school, where she'd finished her master's degree and was about midway through her PhD. He'd actually viewed her college transcripts, as well as her Minnesota driver's license, and the apartment lease from when she moved to Rochester.

Then, with considerable apprehension, he'd searched the social media sites. As it turned out, her profiles and entries were relatively sparse and almost ridiculously

G-rated. Rather than questionable proclivities or embarrassing photos, the sites revealed a sweet, wholesome young woman with an interest in science classes, Christian music, ice skating and children with cancer.

His relief was enormous.

"Okay, enough about me." She took a sip of her Coke. "Your turn. Your experiences have got to be much more exciting than mine. Growing up in Minnesota and working in hospitals are not the height of adventure."

Luke shrugged. "No, not really. I'm just an ordinary guy from a big family in west Texas who wanted to land fighter jets on aircraft carriers. I got halfway there, but then fate—or rather genes—took over and that dream was quashed, leaving me to wander the world at the whim of the U.S. Navy."

She leaned forward, watching his expression as he talked. "I'm sorry. What happened?"

He grinned and rubbed his thumb in the crease between her eyes as if to erase her frown. "Honey, it was probably for the best. What happened is that I was not quite eighteen when I graduated from high school. At that point I was kind of—um—husky, but not all that tall. During my freshman year at the Naval Academy, I grew more than three inches and put on about forty pounds; the next year I grew almost as much. It's rare to see a fighter pilot over six feet tall. Any more than that, and they're at risk of breaking both femurs if they have to eject. I'm fond of my femurs, so, long story short, the Navy found other uses for me."

"What kind of uses?"

"Football for starters. I played for four years while I was in school."

She nodded. "I have no trouble visualizing you playing football. What position?"

"About the least glamorous on the field—offensive line."

"I bet you were good."

"I was okay," he replied.

"I don't believe you. I bet you were amazing!" She chuckled. "You sure look the part." Claire took a sip of her soft drink. "So, besides football, what other uses did the Navy find for you?"

"Computers." He said the word, then finished off his pizza.

"Computers?" She looked doubtful. "You mean the Navy has *you* working on computers?"

"Well, yeah. You seem surprised." Shaking his head and looking downcast, he groaned, "Once again, I'm perceived as a lummox… Just brawn; no brains."

She giggled. "I didn't mean that. I know you're involved with surveillance and I can certainly see you flying planes and piloting ships or doing military police-type stuff. But…computers?" She shook her head. "Not so obvious."

He responded with a wry, almost apologetic look. "I have degrees in computer science and computer engineering—both hardware and software. Believe it or not, I'm a bona fide computer geek."

His nonchalance was charming. "Well, I'm very impressed. That's not easy. I'll have to remember that when I'm having problems with my internet connections." She folded her napkin and moved to a different topic. "You said you came from a 'big family.' Were you talking numbers or…em…stature?"

"Both, I suppose. I have three brothers and a sister, so there are five of us altogether." He chuckled. "I'm the tallest, but my brother Mark is at least six-five, then my oldest brother, Matt, is probably heavier than I am. My youngest brother, John, and sister, Ruthie, are more normal—they take after Mom's side of the family."

"So, you're in the middle then?"

"Yep. We're all about two years apart. Johnny, the baby, just turned twenty-four. He and I are the only ones not married. Everyone else is contributing to the population explosion, making Mom really happy." He pulled out his cell phone and punched a couple of apps. He leaned toward Claire and showed her a family picture. "This was taken when I was home last Christmas. That's Mom and Dad." He indicated the tall, lanky man with gray hair standing by a relatively petite blonde woman. "That's Matt and his wife, Heather, and their three kids. This is Mark and his wife, Kim, and their two little girls, and that is

Ruthie and her husband, Ike. Ruthie was pregnant in the picture; she had a little boy about two months ago… That's me of course, and next to me is Johnny."

"Oh my *gosh!*" Claire exclaimed as she studied the photo. He hadn't been exaggerating. The smallest of the Llewellyn men was the youngest son and he was probably at least six-two. "Your poor mother! She looks tiny surrounded by all of you. How in the world did she give birth to four men as big as you?"

He grinned. "Well, we were smaller then."

"Okay, you got me there." She laughed. "I bet your grocery bills were outrageous!"

"Yeah, but according to both Mom and Dad, the worst part was keeping us all in jeans and athletic shoes. Then there was paying for the car insurance when we started driving… That was brutal." His smile was disarming.

Claire shook her head. "I can only imagine." She was charmed by his affection and pride for his family. "That sounds like so much fun. I always envied people from big families…" Her voice was wistful.

Luke was staring again, but he seemed to have stopped caring.

"So what part of Texas is home?"

"Midland. It's a big town several hundred miles west of Dallas."

"Will you go back there when you leave the Navy?"

He glanced away, suddenly seeming a bit nervous, before his eyes returned to meet hers. "Ahem… Funny you should mention that." His mouth tightened. "The answer is 'yes,' I'm planning on going home to Midland."

"Is something wrong?" Claire asked.

He paused a breath before answering, "The timing stinks."

Claire's brow creased. "Timing?"

"It's only about two weeks."

"What's two weeks?"

"I'm being discharged. I'm heading home in a couple of weeks." He didn't look particularly happy about the prospect.

Claire's disappointment was acute. She folded and refolded her napkin as she struggled to come up with a response. "Oh, I see," she said. "That's great. I'm very happy for you… I know that what you do—well, what you've been doing for years—must be very difficult—being so far from home and all…" She felt like crying.

Luke seemed oddly heartened by her response and managed a grin. "Hey, don't look like that, Mary Claire." He placed one large hand behind her head and rubbed her cheek with his thumb. Holding her eyes with his, he said quietly, "I know we've only known each other for a few days, but there's no way I'm going to let a little thing like you being in Seoul and me being in Texas stop what I think—what I hope— is happening." Very gently, he leaned forward and kissed her temple.

She stared into his hazel eyes, searching for evidence that he felt something akin to the warmth growing in her. Blinking rapidly to fend off threatening tears, Claire spoke softly. Her words were hopeful and tentative. "Yes. All right." She stumbled verbally before recovering. "Well, yes… Please, let's not let a little thing like three thousand miles get in the way." Then she smiled and leaned forward. Almost copying his earlier action, she tentatively kissed his cheek.

The pizza and cheesecake were gone and the waiter approached them with a check. Claire glanced around and noticed that the crowd had dwindled considerably. She looked at her watch and realized they'd been talking for more than two hours.

"Do you need to get home?" Luke asked.

"No, not at all."

"I could stand to work off some of the pizza. Let's go walk down Itaewon and find a coffee shop."

The night air was cool and dry, and even though it was a weekday, the street was very busy. Luke caught Claire's hand to pull her aside, away from a pedestrian who was paying more attention to a heated discussion than his surroundings. The man would have bumped into her, otherwise. When the small threat was over, however, Luke didn't release her, and Claire happily clasped his warm hand. Leisurely they strolled a few blocks down the street and found a Starbucks. Reluctantly, Luke dropped Claire's hand to open the door and ushered her inside.

They collected cups of steaming coffee and found an empty table in a corner. Between sips Luke casually asked, "Have you been paying attention to your surroundings like you promised?"

"Yes, sir. I have, sir." Claire's tone was a bit mocking, but she shifted a little and looked pensive. "Actually, I meant to mention earlier…em…I saw a man this morning. He was outside of our apartment building."

Luke straightened a bit and suddenly looked serious. "What did he look like?"

"He was just a guy slouching against a window across the street from our building. It's odd that I even spotted him because at any given time there must be dozens of men milling around the apartment. It's a very busy area."

"What was it about that guy that made you notice him?"

"I'm not sure." She frowned slightly. "I imagine it's just me being super paranoid since the attack. He didn't do or say anything; he was probably just waiting for someone…"

"Claire, what made you notice him?" Luke repeated.

She stirred her coffee and continued to fiddle with her spoon. "He seemed to be watching me."

"What do you mean?"

"I don't know… I'm sure it's nothing. I probably shouldn't have mentioned it." She knew she sounded a bit exasperated and cupped her hands around her coffee mug.

But Luke was relentless. He reached across the table to hold her hands. "What do you mean that he seemed to be watching you?"

"I felt that his eyes were following me. It was just an odd feeling; I guess maybe like a kind of intuition."

Claire bit her lip, remembering when similar bouts of intuition had proven to be accurate.

"What did he look like?"

"He was Korean," Claire said. "Medium height, about one sixty, with black hair and brown eyes… Probably in his thirties… And I've just described about two million men in Seoul."

Luke rubbed his eyes and sighed. "Did he follow you or anything?"

"No. I took the subway this morning. I noticed him because he seemed to be watching me as I walked to the subway stop. I just— He made me nervous. I crossed the street and glanced back and he was still staring at me and kind of scowling, but he hadn't moved. I just kept going and got on the subway. I didn't see him again and honestly, I forgot about him until you asked." She shook her head and gave a dismissive wave. "I'm sure it was nothing but my active imagination fueled by your suspicions."

Frowning, Luke rubbed her fingers with his thumb. "Honey, please do me a favor. Pay attention to your intuition and my suspicions." His hand squeezed hers and he shook his head. "I just wish I had a clue why someone might be stalking you…" He thought a moment then inquired, "At work—you're not involved in any drug trials, are you?"

"Luke, no! And you've seen for yourself, the playroom is completely benign— well except for some video games rated

PG-13. There's nothing anyone could be angry about. There are no copyrights or products or ideas that have been stolen…"

"Could it be related to Jessica and whatever it is she does at the university?"

"No, that really is far-fetched. Jessica studies Korean culture—specifically the evolution of relationships between men and women. She focuses on courtship and gender roles—that sort of thing. She dates several different guys, none too seriously that I'm aware of. And she's been here for several years. Besides, that has nothing to do with me."

He drummed his fingers on the table and tried another approach. "How about your ice skating? Did you trounce some poor Korean girl in a competition one time, and her father still carries a grudge?"

Claire couldn't hold back a snicker. "Luke, that's ridiculous. I only competed internationally once. That was in Europe and I came in something like fifteenth. Plus, I haven't skated in almost ten years!"

He sighed audibly. "Okay, I give up for now. But please keep on the alert, and if you happen to see that guy again, try to get a picture."

"Okay." She smiled at his persistence. "I've got my smartphone, and a picture wouldn't be hard, but what good would that do?"

He gave her an inscrutable look. "Suffice it to say that facial recognition software has come a long way."

She blinked and bit her lip. "The guys from Friday night... Did you... Could you—"

He shook his head. "No. That was another reason I'm concerned. Between one guy wearing a hoodie and the other guy with a baseball cap pulled down, we couldn't get a good enough capture of either man's features to make identification. It was like they knew how to camouflage just enough to frustrate the software but avoid suspicion."

"Oh" was her only response.

"Just be careful, okay?" Luke sighed and stood. "I don't want this to end, but I probably need to get you home. I've gotta go to Panmunjeom in the morning, and I'm sure you get to the hospital pretty early."

Claire followed Luke as he wove his way among the coffeehouse patrons and through the door. He caught her hand as they proceeded down the crowded street in the direction of his borrowed car. Glancing down at her, he said, "Okay, so tomorrow evening…same time?"

"Please." She smiled for the first time in a while. "I'd love that."

"Maybe burgers? I know a place."

She giggled and held his hand tighter. "I'm sure you do!"

During the twenty-minute drive to Jessica's apartment, Luke told Claire about growing up in a big family in west Texas, and she shared stories from her life in Minnesota. Although he knew the area where Jessica's apartment was, Claire had to direct him to the correct street. As they turned a corner near the building, they were suddenly brought to a stop, blocked by several police cars with lights flashing.

"That's our building," Claire said. She strained to get a better look. "I wonder what's happened."

They were still a block away but couldn't proceed any farther. A uniformed officer had stopped traffic to allow an ambulance to leave the area. The ambulance snaked through the vehicles and passed them. Shortly thereafter, its siren sounded and it was able to pick up speed. After the ambulance's departure, the police officer allowed the cars to progress, and Luke was able to find a parking place close to the apartment building.

As they walked to the entrance, they were stopped by two officers who demanded identification in stilted English. Luke handed over his military ID card and Claire presented her Samsung Medical Center badge. The men seemed to look at her with suspicion, and her already considerable apprehension grew. The officers stared at Luke with concern—no doubt trying to gauge how many policemen it would take to constrain him, should the need arise. Their surreptitious glances might have been comical if she'd had a better understanding of what was happening.

One of the officers studied both identification cards then said something in Korean.

"I'm sorry. English, please," Luke answered.

The man nodded and signaled for them to follow him toward one of the patrol cars. "Come."

"What is it?" Claire asked the officer. She was growing more concerned by the moment.

He pointed to a spot by the car and said, "Stay here." He turned to two other officers and they had a quick, subdued discussion, maintaining watchful—and anxious—eyes on Luke.

The policeman who seemed to have rank pulled out a cell phone and made a quick call, then turned back to the Americans. "Detective come now." He pointed to the building and gestured once more for them to remain where they were.

Claire glanced up at Luke and saw that he was taking in the scene. It seemed as if he was watching for something. He'd pulled her close and was shielding her with his body. She felt dwarfed by him and couldn't see anything but his wide back and shoulders. She stood on her toes, trying to get closer. "What do you think?" she whispered.

"I don't know," he answered almost idly.

Luke squeezed her hand but didn't look at her. He continued to scour the area. "We'll just wait here for their detective. I figure he'll want to ask us some questions."

They didn't have to wait long. Within a couple of minutes, a suited man approached from the building's entrance. The officer handed him their identification and motioned to where they stood. After perusing both IDs a moment, the newcomer came forward. Luke was still blocking Claire, so the man addressed him first. In passable English, he said, "Lieutenant. I am Detective Kang, of Seoul National University precinct."

He nodded toward Claire, who was largely obscured by Luke's bulk. "You are Miss Olsen." Claire peered around Luke, and he grudgingly stepped aside.

"Yes, I'm Mary Claire Olsen," she answered quietly.

"Miss Olsen, there has been an incident here. I must ask you questions."

"What kind of incident?" Luke didn't seem willing to allow the detective access to Claire without more information.

"There has been attack." Detective

Kang tried—mostly successfully—to not look intimidated by the American man. He glanced down at a clipboard and then moved his gaze from Luke to pin Claire directly. "Doctor Tyson was attacked. She is hurt very bad."

Claire responded with a panicked "*Jessica!*" Luke quickly pulled her into a loose embrace.

"How badly? What happened?" Claire's face felt flushed. The volume of her voice rose as she pointed to the street. "Was she in that ambulance? Will she be okay?" She practically squeaked as she bombarded the detective with questions.

Detective Kang looked at Luke rather pleadingly, then answered, "Two men were in her apartment. She was hit and choked. Men tried to push her from window but she cried out." He looked glum. "She go to University Hospital—very near."

Claire ceased straining at Luke's grasp. Her heart was thudding painfully and she was crying. "I need to go… Which way? Where is the hospital?"

The detective put up his hand. "No. First you come to station for questions."

"Is that necessary?" Luke interjected. "Miss Olsen is very concerned for her friend... Also, she's recovering from being attacked herself last week."

Detective Kang gave Luke an inscrutable look. "Yes, Lieutenant. I know about the Friday attack. That is why we must talk." Their eyes held and Luke felt a chill run down his spine as he considered the possible implications of those words.

CHAPTER SEVEN

LUKE WOULDN'T LET Claire out of his sight. Rather than argue with him and risk some sort of altercation, Detective Kang allowed Luke to accompany her to the station. They didn't speak during the brief trip, but Claire wouldn't let go of Luke's hand. He was concerned about her, as she was seemingly in worse condition than the previous weekend when *she'd* been the victim.

By the time Claire and Luke were ushered into the police station, it was after ten o'clock. They followed Detective Kang to an office with glass walls that was surrounded by a large work area. The detective seated the Americans, then spoke to a subordinate for a moment before sitting behind the wide metal desk. The entire scene was eerily reminiscent of the previous Saturday at the embassy. But this time, Luke was sitting next to Claire, supporting her.

They waited only a short time before another suited man joined them, introducing himself as Captain Choi. The captain started the questioning. "Miss Olsen, where were you tonight?"

She licked her lips and answered. "I work at the Samsung Medical Center. I was there until about 5:30. Lieutenant Llewellyn picked me up and we went to dinner." Her voice seemed to grow a little stronger, and she glanced askance at Luke before returning her attention to the captain.

At the policemen's prompting, Claire recounted their evening, including the time frame and places she and Luke had gone— all of which were easily verifiable. Then she was asked to describe the events of the previous Friday evening. The captain listened attentively and the detective took notes throughout the inquiry.

Luke remained silent as Claire gave them her account. He suspected the officers already knew most of what she told them. As their questioning progressed, Luke had a suspicion the time when she would need him was fast approaching.

The policemen asked Claire many of the same questions Luke had brought up during his interrogation. Like him, they were evidently struggling to discern the reason for that attack. With all of their questions answered, Detective Kang looked at his superior for direction. Receiving a nod, he addressed Claire. "Miss Olsen, you need details of attack on Dr. Tyson."

Luke could tell that Claire was trying desperately to retain her composure. She had been sitting very straight and answering the questions quietly. She was clearly worried about Jessica and anxious to finish the interview so she could go to the hospital.

Captain Choi took over the discussion. "A neighbor was alerted by a scream coming from Dr. Tyson's apartment about eight o'clock. There were crashing noises and a window was broken. The neighbor called the building's security guard, who called police. The guard knew that no visitors had checked in to see Dr. Tyson, so he did not know who the assailant might be. He went to the apartment, but when the elevator door opened, he saw two men running toward the stairs. He did not get a good look. He entered the apartment and saw Miss Tyson on the floor. She was conscious but injured."

Claire swallowed and nodded. "Do you know who they were?" Her voice was very quiet.

"No. They had entered the building earlier in the afternoon acting as television cable men for another resident." He looked down at the draft of the report, then returned his gaze to her. "Dr. Tyson arrived at about seven thirty, so they waited for her much of the day."

"Did the men attack Jessica over her work?" Claire looked confused then glanced at Luke. Had his hypothesis been correct?

Luke's expression impassive, but his hands were tightly fisted.

"We are still gathering clues, but there is something else, Miss Olsen." The captain looked at Claire with curiosity, and the way he said the words made Luke sit up straighter, sensing that what was coming was critical. "Dr. Tyson was wearing a black wig and glasses when she arrived at home this evening. The detective thought that was strange, but the doorman assured him that Dr. Tyson wore them often. Can you give us more information?"

Claire's frown deepened, but she answered without pause. "Jessica studies dating relationships between Korean men and women. She told me her blond hair attracts a lot of unwanted attention, so wearing the black wig and glasses helps her blend in. She can observe couples and talk more openly if it's a little less obvious that she's an American... Do you think *that* has something to do with why she was attacked?" Her hand was shaking as she brushed her hair aside and asked again, "Do you think someone was angry over her work?"

"No, Miss Olsen," the detective answered. He seemed genuinely concerned. "The attack on Dr. Tyson was mistake. We know two men waiting for you—think Dr. Tyson is you."

Claire was stunned. Her eyes grew huge, and she paled. Luke reached over to take her hand. "You're certain of this?"

he asked. It was the first he'd spoken since meeting the captain.

"Yes," the captain said. "Dr. Tyson was awake when the police arrived. She told the first officer that the men thought they were attacking Miss Olsen until they pulled off her wig and realized she had blond hair." He kept his eyes on Luke as he provided additional details. "It seems they were trying to push her out of the window—perhaps to resemble a suicide, when they discovered they had the wrong woman. They were very angry when they learned of the error, and that is when they harmed Dr. Tyson. They wanted her to tell them where to find Miss Olsen. They broke one arm and blackened her eye."

Unable to stifle a sob, Claire doubled over, clutching her stomach. All three men were startled, and after a moment Luke stood and pulled her into a comforting embrace. He pressed her face to his chest and gave the other men a warning look. "I think that is enough for now. Ms. Olsen has had a series of difficult shocks. I need to take her home."

The captain shook his head. "No. Even

if she could go home, it is not advisable. There will be forensic teams there for many more hours." He looked as if he was hesitant to say more but decided that it was necessary. "Also, do not overlook that whoever is trying to harm her has made two attempts. They know where she lives and where she works."

"I know." Luke felt himself tense, as if he were preparing to fend off a challenge. His voice was mild however as he offered, "It's okay. I'll take care of her. I'll take her to Yongsan."

The captain was not going to argue. He nodded and gave Luke a brief smile. "Yes, that will be good. I think she will be safe with you." His smile faded and he shook his head a bit ominously. Although he was looking at Claire, he continued to address Luke. "She will not be allowed to leave the country, however. I will put a hold on her passport and exit visa."

Luke wondered if the man had read his mind. He paused a breath before responding. "Captain, someone has tried twice to kill her. The safest place for her is back in the U.S." His stare was intense, and his words were clipped and authoritative.

The older man tried to pacify Luke. "A few days only. Let us finish the investigation. If she stays at Yongsan, most likely whoever is seeking to harm her will not know where she is. But if they learn, their access will be severely hindered." His serious expression grew even more stern when he added, "If she leaves Yongsan, she should be accompanied by an—er—escort." He avoided using the term "bodyguard," but the implication was obvious.

Luke pressed his lips together, but he gave a very brief nod of acquiescence. "Okay. But only for a few days. Also, I'm going to call our embassy and make them aware of the situation for both Dr. Tyson and Miss Olsen."

"I agree. That is wise."

Claire seemed to pay little attention to the exchange. At the end of the conversation she faced the two men and said, "Jessica. Please, can I go to the hospital to see Jessica."

Luke continued to hold Claire, giving her protection and support. "Would you instruct someone to take us by the hospital on the way back to my car?"

The captain nodded solemnly. "Yes. We will ensure that officers accompany you to the hospital and follow you to the base."

CLAIRE AND LUKE were taken to Seoul National University Hospital accompanied by Detective Kang and a uniformed officer. With the policemen's assistance, they cut through the red tape preventing after-hours visitation.

Much to Claire's relief, another uniformed policeman was guarding Jessica's room. With Detective Kang acting as interpreter, Claire spoke with the night nurse. Jessica had suffered simple fractures to both bones in her right forearm. The arm was currently encased in a soft splint and would be casted in a few days, after the swelling had resolved. She'd been struck several times around her face, and her right eye was blackened. Fortunately, a CT-scan had showed there was no permanent damage. The nurse explained that Jessica had been brought to the room about half an hour before, and per the doctor's orders she'd been given a fairly strong sedative and was sleeping.

Finally inside her friend's room, Claire felt her chest constrict. A very wan Jessica was lying in the bed in an ugly hospital gown, but all the monitors indicated that she was doing well. An IV was dripping slowly into a needle in Jessica's left arm, and her splinted right arm was propped on a pillow at her side. A small ice bag had been placed over her injured eye, and Claire lifted the bag and winced slightly when she saw the swelling and bruising. Jessica was sleeping soundly and didn't appear to be in any pain. Claire replaced the ice bag and gently patted her uninjured hand. "I'll come back to see you tomorrow," she whispered. She nodded to the nurse and said, "*Kamsahamnida*."

LUKE HAD WAITED outside Jessica's room with the guard. When Claire rejoined them, he saw that she was desperately trying to hold back tears, and he also recognized signs of fatigue. He badly wanted to pull her into an embrace and remove her from any more ugliness, but he controlled that impulse. Glancing at his watch, he saw it was after midnight. The best thing now would be getting her someplace she could rest.

The captain had instructed the officers to allow Luke and Claire to enter the apartment, so that she could collect some of her clothes and personal items. A small team of forensic experts and police were still present, but Luke was relieved to see that there didn't seem to be extensive damage or visible blood. Luke remained at her side as they entered the unit, hoping to forestall exposure to distressing evidence. One window was shattered and some of the furniture was displaced. A picture and mirror had been broken, but otherwise, the apartment seemed to be in pretty good shape. Luke followed Claire to her room, where she quickly filled a suitcase with clothing and toiletries. In less than five minutes she was ready to leave.

As they started to go, she remembered something else. "My laptop. I'd like to take my computer with me," she said.

The detective shook his head. "No. Sorry, Miss Olsen. Your computer taken to police station. Forensic team will look for clues. Will return very soon."

She seemed to take a few seconds to process the statement. Finally she nodded. "Okay. That's fine, but I would like to get it back soon. I have a lot of my work on it."

Luke had been dismayed by that development, as he would've liked access to Claire's computer—to scour it for clues—but he kept silent. Throughout the ordeal, he'd managed to remain calm and supportive, fully knowing that was what Claire needed. Inwardly, however, he was seething. He was sorry that Jessica had been injured, although her injuries were not overly serious. What infuriated him was that two men had tried to do serious bodily injury to Claire twice in less than a week. Indeed, it was becoming increasingly clear to him, that both attacks had been attempted murder. Only tenacity and athletic ability on Claire's part had thwarted the first attack and the second had been forestalled by luck.

He shuddered to think what would have happened had he not taken her to dinner. She would have come back to the apartment alone and been at the mercy of the two men. Luke knew that they would likely have succeeded in killing her this time.

Jessica had been spared because she was not Claire, and the men were trying to get information from her. He didn't know what they'd been able to extract during the brutal attack. Had Jessica mentioned *his* name as she was being threatened and beaten? If so, they might have a hint as to where to look for Claire. Luke really didn't care if they came after him, but he didn't like knowing they might be able to locate Claire through him.

What he really wanted—badly—was to go straight to Incheon Airport and put Claire on the first plane bound for the United States. But it looked like that wouldn't be an option—not until the police allowed her to leave. For the time being, Claire needed to remain with him. Now came the tricky part—convincing Claire.

He took the bag from her and led her to the door. "Do you have everything you need?"

"Yes, I think so." Her voice was quiet. "I wish I could have my laptop, though. I need it to communicate with my parents and I use it for my school work and my work at Mayo…"

Luke led her into the elevator and pressed the button for the ground floor. "Don't worry about that. I have computers you can use."

They exited the elevator, and the police followed them through the building and down the block to collect Luke's car. In a short time they were headed to Yongsan. Luke glanced at Claire and saw that fatigue, worry and fear were definitely taking their toll. She looked like she was having trouble concentrating. Despite being slightly obscured by her glasses, dark circles were evident under red-rimmed eyes. "Luke, I'm so sorry to have dragged you into this. You've been wonderful and I don't know what I would have done if you hadn't been with me…" Twin tears slipped down her cheeks.

"Mary Claire, don't cry. Jessica's going to be fine. We'll figure this out." He couldn't refrain from gently caressing her wet cheek with his fingers.

She swiped at her eyes and tried to

smile. "I've already imposed on you too much, Luke. I know what you told the captain—that you were going to take me to Yongsan. But that isn't necessary. I can go to a hotel." Her voice sounder stronger than before.

"Not a *chance!*"

Claire started when he all but shouted his objection. Contrition swiftly followed and he took her hand, forcing himself to calm down.

"No, it *is* necessary, honey. There are several options when we get you to Yongsan. There's a hotel on base, although it's often overbooked, particularly this time of year. But we can check. I also have several friends who have extra room, or—" he tilted her chin until she had to meet his eyes "—you can stay with me."

She blinked several times and looked away.

"Claire, I'm not suggesting that you stay with *me*, per se, but you can stay in my apartment, at least for the next few days. I share quarters with an Air Force captain who's away right now ferrying a plane to the Middle East. He'll be gone for at least a week. The apartment has two bedrooms and two bathrooms. You can take Brad's room until we get this all figured out, or barring that, get you back home."

Shock and fatigue had dulled Claire's inclination to argue. Wiping away her tears, she blessed him with a watery smile and a hesitant nod. "Okay, but only for a day or two. And I promise to stay out of your way."

DURING THE DRIVE TO YONGSAN, Claire was too tired to talk, so Luke told her about the base. "Yongsan Army Garrison is the home of the U.S. Eighth Army in Korea," he said. "It's actually really large—more than one square mile—and it's located at almost the dead center of Seoul."

She nodded absently and continued to stare at the sparse early-morning traffic.

"The city was decimated during the Korean War," Luke continued. "Only a few of the larger buildings were left intact and the inhabitants had scattered. Over time, the country grew and modernized, and Seoul's population exploded. The city grew around the base. Now Yongsan houses about eight thousand people. There are all sorts of housing complexes, schools, grocery stores, a hospital and theaters, in addition to office buildings.

"It's safe," Luke said as they neared a gate. "The garrison is surrounded by a fifteen foot concrete wall, topped with razor wire, and all the entrances are manned by armed personnel from the U.S. and Korean military."

At the gate, Claire was required to complete a brief form, relinquish her temporary passport and be fingerprinted, before being given a base pass. It was after one o'clock when Luke finally unlocked the door to his apartment and ushered a very tired and somewhat wary Claire inside.

Luke flipped a light switch, revealing a relatively generous combination living and dining room. She could see a small kitchen behind the dining area. The living space was traditionally furnished, consisting of a comfortable-looking, but somewhat worn leather sofa and a couple of upholstered chairs, along with coffee and end tables. A flat-screened TV adorned one wall. The dining area looked as if it was rarely used for eating, as the table was littered with an impressive assortment of computer towers, monitors and laptops.

Luke pointed to his left. "That's my room." He moved in the other direction, leading her to a closed door. "Brad's room is this way." He opened the door and peered in. "I don't normally go in here," he said. "He's a good guy and pretty neat for the most part." He grinned a little sheepishly. "I hope—but don't guarantee—there won't be any surprises under the bed."

He flipped on a light, revealing a bedroom furnished with twin beds. A nightstand was located between the beds and two dressers lined the near wall. A small closet could be seen beyond the beds and another door led to a bathroom on the far wall, away from the living area. The room was meticulously neat. Only a few books and some sports equipment, along with framed pictures and other small personal items, gave any indication that it was currently inhabited.

Luke gestured toward the first bed. "Brad sleeps there, and I imagine, or at least I hope, that the sheets on the other bed are clean…" He placed her bag on his roommate's bed then crossed the brief space to pull back the covers on the far bed, revealing a bare mattress and pillow. "Hmm…" he mumbled and then strode to the far dresser and opened drawers. The top three were empty, but he found what he was seeking in the last drawer, removing a set of clean, folded sheets. He placed them on the bed then turned to Claire. She was still standing at the door, as if she were afraid to enter.

Luke crossed the room and lightly touched her arm. "Claire, what is it? Is something wrong?"

At that moment Claire was incapable of answering. She simply stared and tried to come up with a way to thank him without revealing the truth behind her cascading emotions. His earnest consideration had crushed the remaining fragments of the carefully maintained barrier that had protected her heart. She was left open and vulnerable.

Luke had been as steady as a rock throughout the ordeal. He'd been quiet, unassuming and undemanding. As she watched the handsome, strong, intelligent man puttering around the room trying to ensure that she had clean sheets, she realized she'd been teetering on the edge of being in love with him since she'd watched him sitting on the floor playing with the sick children the previous day. The fall had been rapid and painless on her part. And, at that moment, she was so totally in love with this man that she was left speechless.

Substituting actions for the words that escaped her, she took two steps in his direction and held up her arms. He caught her, gently enveloping her in a tender embrace, somehow sensing what she needed. She buried her face in his shoulder and grasped his shirt with both hands, clinging like she would never let go.

The hard muscles of Luke's chest and arms encased Claire with reassurance and protection. She felt his hands move gently up her back, soothing her. He lightly kissed the top of her head and her heart clutched again, beating erratically as she continued the downward slide into total adoration. She stifled a sob and held on tighter.

"Shush… Mary Claire, what is it? Are you still frightened? It's going to be okay. I promise, nothing will happen to you," he whispered into her hair. Luke held her for a while, soothing and rocking her. Finally, he pulled away a bit. He eased off her glasses and set them on the dresser, and then he put his huge hands on each side of her head and raised her face up, urging her to look at him. Tentatively her eyes rose to his.

Ever so tenderly, Luke's thumb caressed her lips. When she didn't tense, he leaned down, watching her carefully. Just as his lips touched hers, her eyes closed and she rose on her toes. Her arms reached up, encircling his neck as she pulled him down, trying to get even closer.

Luke shook himself slightly and pulled back. He kept both hands on her shoulders, as if reluctant to completely break the embrace.

He took a deep breath and murmured, "Well, wow. It looks like we're going to have more to talk about tomorrow." He swallowed hard and tried to smile. Finally, he dropped his hands and stepped back.

"But for now, we both need to get some sleep... You're exhausted and I have an early call to go north on patrol." Claire still hadn't said anything, and he hesitated before leaving. "Claire, are you okay? Do you need anything?"

Seconds passed before Claire managed a response. She shuddered slightly and reached out her hand to touch his. "Luke, thank you so much for all you've done for me. I know I'm a bother, but don't worry, I've got all that I need." She motioned to the door and added, "Please go and get some sleep. I'll be fine."

He studied her a moment more and then squeezed her hand slightly. "Seriously, make yourself at home. If you need me, I'm just across the living room..." Finally, with nothing to add, he turned and walked out, closing the door quietly behind him.

Claire sank to the bed, her shaking legs no longer able to support her weight. She stared at the door for several minutes, trying to sort out her tumultuous emotions. A short while later, she rose and crossed the room, picked up the sheets and made the bed. After unpacking a few items and replacing her slacks and sweater with an old T-shirt and boxers, she crawled into the borrowed bed and fell into an exhausted slumber.

CHAPTER EIGHT

WHEN CLAIRE WOKE the next morning, she felt only a moment of disorientation. The room was cool and quiet. The curtains covering the lone window were fairly heavy, but bright sunlight was visible around the edges, suggesting that morning was well underway. Sitting up, Claire glanced at the nightstand between the twin beds and saw the alarm clock was facing the other bed. She turned it to her and was surprised to discover that it was after nine.

"Oh my gosh!" she said out loud and scrambled up. She dressed quickly and performed basic grooming, eager to see Luke. Taking a deep breath, she opened the door leading to the main part of the apartment and found the combination living room and dining room and the kitchen area beyond empty. The door to Luke's room was open and she peered through it cautiously, listening for a sign that he was there. Not hearing anything, she glanced around. Like Brad's, Luke's room was remarkably neat. His bed was made, and other than some books and a pair of really large running shoes, nothing was out of place.

"Luke?" she said, loudly enough to be heard anywhere in the apartment. There was no answer—she was alone. At a loss as to what to do next, she turned back toward the kitchen. Then she spotted a typed note taped to one of the computer monitors.

Mary Claire,
There's food in the fridge and pan-try—help yourself.

This computer is set up for you to use—your password is 'Iceskater'. You should be able to access the internet and do anything you need to do on it.

The black phone is a direct U.S. line. You can call anyone in the U.S.— just dial the area code and number; talk as long as you wish.

Last thing—Sgt. Tony Mancini (from the embassy) will be here at noon to take you to see Jessica. Don't go ANYWHERE off base without him.

I should be back by four or five. Be at home.

He'd scrawled "Luke" at the bottom of the page.

Claire smiled as she reread the note, appreciating his consideration in taking the time to set her up with a computer and make arrangements for her to check on Jessica. She had no idea when he'd left but vaguely recalled him mentioning that he had an early day. He must not have gotten more than a couple of hours' sleep.

She read the note a third time before setting it on the table and looking around the apartment. She sighed quietly and then said out loud, "Well, okay then."

The first thing she did was use her cell phone to call the hospital and explain to her colleagues that she was staying at Yongsan Base and likely wouldn't be in until she could find an escort. Following that, she called her parents. She'd already told them about having her purse stolen, but not wanting to worry them, she didn't mention the knife wound. Claire debated a while about how to describe the latest development and decided to minimize the incident. She explained that she'd decided to move nearer the embassy while waiting for her passport, and said that she was staying in the spare bedroom of one of the embassy workers while the room's occupant was away. Fortunately, her parents were about to go to bed, so they didn't ask for a lot of details.

Breakfast came next. Claire was pleasantly surprised that the fridge and pantry were pretty well stocked. She helped herself to a bowl of Cheerios topped with a sliced banana and a cup of tea. The next couple of hours were spent on the computer and she was amazed by the speed of Luke's equipment. She was easily able to access her school sites and email accounts, so she spent some time working on one of her assignments.

At about 11:45 she logged off and slipped into Brad's room to get ready to see Jessica. She dressed in one of her standard work outfits—a long skirt and lightweight sweater—then pulled her hair up and secured it with a clip. By the time there was a knock at the door, she was anxious and waiting.

Tony Mancini was dressed in his uniform, consisting of a khaki shirt and olive trousers, exactly as he had been when they'd met earlier. He smiled and said, "Good morning, miss."

"Sergeant, thanks so much for coming by and taking me to see Jessica." She smiled gratefully. "I know this isn't part of your normal duties and I hope that it isn't a lot of trouble…."

"No, ma'am. I assure you I was pleased when Luke called this morning to ask if I could take you to see your friend." Humor was apparent in the crinkles of the corners of his chocolate-colored eyes. The smile faded and suddenly his expression turned severe. "Luke told me what happened— about the attack on Dr. Tyson…"

Claire's lips compressed and she blinked several times. "Yes, that was my fault…"

His look softened considerably. "That's not what Luke told me. He said the idiots are still after you, but they messed up and attacked her. That's hardly your fault."

She shook her head and whispered, "Sergeant, I don't know what's going on. Nothing about this makes sense, and I'm horribly sorry that Jessica was involved."

"Well, let's go see her. I'm sure talking to her will do you both good."

Claire picked up her purse and followed the marine to his car. "I don't know how Luke set this all up. I actually haven't talked to him today—he just left me a note that you were coming. When did he call you?"

Tony opened the passenger door for her. "About 6:30."

"You didn't mind him calling at 6:30?"

"Trust me," he said, "we get up early." He settled into the driver's seat and started the vehicle. "Actually, I have second shift today, so I'm off right now. Nothing pressing until later this afternoon." He patted her hand companionably. "Let's go see Ms. Tyson."

DURING THE DRIVE Tony was talkative, trying to put her at ease. Claire learned that he was from New Jersey and had been a Marine for more than fifteen years. He had completed tours in both Iraq and Afghanistan, and finally, after multiple deployments, he'd landed the relatively cushy and highly sought after job of Embassy Security. Tony was gregarious and funny, and by the time they arrived at the hospital, he and Claire were friends.

AT THE HOSPITAL, Tony stayed within arm's reach, so when Claire walked into Jessica's room he was at her side. Seeing her friend sitting up in the bed with her broken arm propped on a pillow and one eye nearly swollen shut, Claire couldn't prevent a sob as she rushed to the bed.

"Oh, Jessica. I'm so sorry…"

Jessica held out her hand and managed a comforting smile. "Claire…girl, it wasn't your fault!"

"Yes it was! Detective Kang said they thought you were me! And then when they found out you weren't, then they…they hurt you…"

Soon both women were crying and hugging and trying to console each other.

When they finally pulled apart, Claire found a tissue and dried her eyes. Belatedly, she remembered Tony. She motioned to him and said, "Oh, Jessica, I forgot. I brought a friend—well actually, he brought me. You remember Sergeant Mancini?"

Tony held out his hand to take Jessica's good one in a friendly shake. The look in his eye was the antithesis of friendly, however, as he studied Jessica's injuries. Claire was alarmed by the tension in his jaw and his cold, piercing eyes. He swore quietly before dropping her hand and stepping back. His face instantly lost the furious stare, but his lips pushed together in a frown. Claire got the impression that if the men who'd harmed Jessica were in the room, they'd face an unenviable fate at the hands of Sergeant Mancini.

Turning back to her friend, Claire sat on the edge of the bed. "Okay, tell me what all they've told you. Are they taking good care of you here?"

Jessica grinned. "I assume you want all the gory details." She glanced at her arm and looked relieved. "Fortunately, the break was very simple—'non-displaced' they called it. And my face will just look bad for a while." Tears formed briefly in her good eye, but she managed to keep her smile. "Nothing broken there, fortunately."

"How long will you be hospitalized?"

"I'll be discharged tomorrow. I'm still working out where I'm going, since I've been told that I can't go home."

Claire looked at her with renewed contrition. "I know, I'm sorry…"

"Claire, it's not your fault. Anyway, it may take a while to get the window replaced, and the police don't want me to go back until this is all figured out…"

"So where do you think you'll stay?"

"I've got a couple of friends in the Anthropology Department who've offered. The university also has a hotel, but I kind of don't want to be alone."

"I wish I could come stay with you, but I'm supposed to stay at the base, at least for the time being."

"Good. That's the perfect place." She smiled conspiringly. "I'm sure that Lieutenant Luke will keep you safe."

The friends talked for more than an hour. After a while they pulled Tony into the conversation and soon he had them laughing. A little after 2:00 Tony said, "Ladies, I truly hate to break this up, but I have to get Claire back to Yongsan and head to the embassy for my shift."

Obediently, Claire rose. She held Jessica's good hand for a moment and said, "Take care. Call me if you need anything or get bored."

As they were leaving, Tony looked uncharacteristically awkward. He returned to the bed. His demeanor suddenly turned serious and he handed Jessica a card. "Here's my contact information. Call me if and when you need anything—really." His eyes were steady on hers.

Watching from the door, Claire saw Jessica swallow and blink quickly before she managed a brief nod. "Thank you, Tony. When you can, that is, if you can…um… you might come back…"

"Count on it." He nodded, then turned to collect Claire and accompany her to the Army base. The warmth was back in Tony's eyes.

CHAPTER NINE

CLAIRE WAS SURPRISED to find Luke waiting at the apartment when they returned. He had apparently been working at the dining room-computer center, and rose to greet them when Tony opened the door.

Luke eyed Claire admiringly and gave her a smile. Then he offered Tony his hand. "Thanks, man. Did you have any problems?"

"Nope. All was quiet. I didn't see anything suspicious," Tony replied.

"Well, I greatly appreciate it. Thanks again—I owe you," Luke said.

Tony briefly shook his head. "No, I don't think so." His smile was a bit sly. "I think that maybe, I'm going to owe you."

Luke looked puzzled but Tony only grinned then shook Claire's hand, as well. The handshake turned into a brief hug. "Tony, thanks tons. You were great."

"It was my pleasure. Glad I could help out." He gave a brief salute to Luke. "See you later," he said and left.

Luke closed the door and turned to Claire. "What was that about?" He looked a little confused and maybe even a bit jealous.

Claire shrugged and her lips curled into a smile. "I think there was a bit of a mutual 'something' between Tony and Jessica. It wouldn't surprise me if... Well, who knows?"

With Luke's full attention on her, Claire suddenly felt awkward. Instead of his 'office' uniform of black slacks and a khaki shirt, Luke was dressed in camouflaged fatigues. The change of attire was oddly disconcerting and made him seem even larger. She wasn't sure what to do—should she hug him? Shake his hand?

Finally, she asked, "Um...when did you get home?"

"About half an hour ago. Since I had to leave early this morning and didn't get to see you, I wanted to get back." He seemed a little uncomfortable, too.

She walked to him then and lightly

touched his hand with her fingers. "Luke, thank you so much for that." She gestured toward the door. "I mean for calling Tony and helping me to go see Jessica." She bit her lip. "That was special. It was really important to me because I wanted to check on her."

A little tentatively, he raised his hand to stroke her cheek. His voice was quiet and deeper than normal when he repeated Tony's words. "It was my pleasure." His eyes were serious as they searched hers.

They were so close. Both knew that the next move was hers. She could step one inch closer and be in his embrace, or she could take a step back and break the spell. Several moments passed before she gave a small sound, broke the contact and took a step in retreat.

Luke seemed simultaneously relieved and devastated. He blinked and then turned toward the kitchen. "How about something to drink? I was going to get a Coke. Can I get you one, too?"

"That would be great." She followed him to the kitchen area and watched as he put ice in glasses and opened two soft drink cans.

He pointed toward the living area. "Here, let's go talk. You can tell me about how Jessica is doing."

Sitting side-by-side on the weathered leather sofa, they chatted about Jessica's recovery and the possibility of a blossoming romance between the professor and the marine. "Well that would just be too weird," Luke commented with a grin. "I've known Tony about a year and he's very much the happy bachelor. I've never seen him act quite like that before."

"You think he's a good guy, don't you?" Claire frowned slightly.

"Yes, he's a good guy. I wouldn't have asked him to take you, if I didn't trust him."

"Oh." Claire's shyness returned and she took a quick sip of the cola. Glancing back up she asked, "Do you have to go back to work?"

"Not officially. I need to keep an eye on some things, but I can do that from here." He nodded toward the group of computers. "I might be called back in, but hopefully all will stay quiet. As I recall, I promised you a hamburger tonight. I thought I could work a while from here and then we could head out to the base's best grill and maybe go to the movies. We get first-run flicks at Yongsan's theater, and the new *Batman* sequel is on."

Her smile was huge. "That sounds fantastic."

ON FRIDAY, Luke made arrangements to take the afternoon shift so he could accompany Claire to the medical center. Over hamburgers the previous evening, she mentioned that she wanted to check on some of the children and do some work, and hesitantly asked if he could help her find an escort. Luke declined her request, insisting that he would take her himself. He'd also loaned Claire one of his laptops so she could transfer her data to coding sheets. With the data downloaded, she'd be able to work on her research project from his apartment.

"ARE YOU SURE this is okay?" Claire asked as she climbed into the aging Honda sedan

Luke had borrowed for the day. "I mean, are you sure you don't need to go in this morning to do your 'day or anytime' job?"

He grinned. "Nope, not a problem. Actually, the guy I switched shifts with was ecstatic. It's Friday and he'd much rather do the early shift and leave his evening open for—well, whatever." He climbed into the driver's seat and headed toward the gate.

"But it messes up your Friday evening..." She still looked worried.

"Yeah, so what?" He shrugged. "I get to spend Friday morning and afternoon with you. We'll worry about Friday evening later."

Luke maneuvered through the crowded city traffic. "Okay, let's set the ground rules," he said casually, glancing at her before returning his attention to the road. "I'll stay with you as much as possible, certainly when you're in public areas. If you need to go to a patient's room or somewhere that's more restricted, be sure to let me know exactly where you'll be and give me some kind of time estimate."

"Luke, of course that's fine, and I'll

follow instructions, but don't you think this is a little overkill? First off, we don't know that they—whoever *they* are—will be watching the hospital. Besides, the hospital is so big and so public, I can't imagine that they would try anything inside..." Skepticism and more than a little frustration was clear in her tone. "And, besides I really hate that you have to take time off to sit around a hospital and look after me. That'll be terribly boring for you."

"Honey," he said, "you just called it— we don't know. They may be watching and they may not. They may try to hurt you again—they may not. But I'm not willing to take a chance." He grinned at her. "And, Claire, I spend hours upon hours staring at computer screens and listening to radio exchanges waiting for something to happen. I'm really good at it. Hanging around a hospital, looking out for you for a few hours is nothing. Besides, I'm counting on a rematch with the boy from the other evening—Min-soo. My reputation has taken a hit; that must be rectified."

Luke maintained a wary and watchful eye as they traversed the parking lot and passed through the automatic doors into the hospital. As before, it was a challenge to try to identify a potential assailant or someone with undue interest in Claire because he himself attracted so many stares. As they proceeded into the large lobby and waiting area, however, his attention was drawn to a lone man sitting near the entrance. The man was holding a magazine in front of his face in an awkward position. He appeared to be reading but could easily observe the entrance. As Luke and Claire walked in, he quickly—and not too stealthily—shifted his attention from the door to the printed pages.

Luke could almost feel his stare. He slipped his smartphone out of his pocket, ready to take a quick picture of the man. When they'd gotten about twenty feet across the lobby, Luke stopped abruptly. Pretending to pick something up, he reached down and glanced behind them, his phone in his hand. He was annoyed to discover, however, that the man had risen from his perch and was moving quickly toward the exit. Luke stood and monitored the man's departure. While he was watching, the stranger glanced back. For a split second their eyes met, then the Korean man turned and hurriedly left the building.

Luke blew out a breath and looked at Claire. She was watching him with curiosity and some concern. "What is it?" she whispered, stepping a little closer.

Luke glanced back to the hospital entrance, where a family of four was now coming in. "Dunno," he said. "But that was interesting." He briefly considered trying to follow the man but didn't want to leave Claire alone.

"What?" Claire's voice was still very quiet.

"Just that guy in the dark blue baseball cap. Did you happen to notice him?"

She shook her head and leaned around him to try and see beyond the wide automatic doors.

"He was in that seat, watching the door, and he seemed nervous to me. Anyway, he hopped up after we went by—maybe he got scared off." Luke took her arm, trying to encourage her to proceed on through the lobby. "Let's go and get you somewhere a little less open. Do you want to go to the playroom first?"

Claire hesitated, still staring at the door.

"Honey, don't worry. Most likely it was nothing—just some guy nervous about hospitals. But if he was one of the bad guys, he knows now you're not alone." He tried his most reassuring look. "Claire, I've got this. Nothing is going to happen to you." He rubbed his thumb lightly to smooth out the lines between her eyebrows. "Come on. Let's get to work."

She took a deep breath and shook her head slightly. "Thank you for being here." Her voice was solemn.

CLAIRE AND LUKE spent most of the morning in the playroom with nearly a score of children, parents and health providers. Claire set up a work station on a small desk in one corner of the large room. There she was able to access the data she needed from each patient's records through the medical center's intranet. She entered the information onto coding sheets she had created earlier, planning to conduct a series of statistical analyses at a later time.

While she was engrossed in her work, Luke was free to entertain the children. He was a little disappointed that Min-soo wasn't present for a rematch, but he was coaxed into games with some of the younger patients. After overcoming their initial apprehension of the giant American, the children were attracted to his natural ease, self-deprecating demeanor and willingness to play.

Claire made excellent progress, although her work was hindered somewhat by laughs, giggles, groans and barks. Unable to ignore the happy sounds, she would look up to see Luke petting a pup, tickling a child, or firing multiple rounds at a projected assailant with a joystick.

Near midmorning, Min-soo joined the group. Luke took in his appearance, expertly noting the subtle changes since he'd seen the adolescent a few days prior. He was now clutching an IV pole and looked quite pale. The boy's wan face brightened, however, when he spotted Luke. "Hey, sir," he said excitedly. "Will you play Angry Birds?"

Luke feigned a punch to the boy's shoulder and replied, "Bud, that's why I'm here. I want a rematch."

Eventually, a small crowd watched as Min-soo won two out of three games. Claire gave up trying to concentrate and joined the group to encourage a dejected Luke as he lost the match. "Well, champ, you got me again," he said admiringly, giving the boy a fist bump. Min-soo beamed.

During the final game, a nurse had entered the room and waited patiently until the end. As they finished, she gave Min-soo a pat on the shoulder and said something to him with visible compassion. She pointed to the door and said something else.

The boy was immediately dejected. He rose, glanced askance at Luke and said something to the nurse, then pointed to the American. The nurse shrugged and looked toward one of the English-speaking therapists, asking him to interpret.

The therapist turned to Luke. "Sir, Min-soo needs to return to his room for a lumbar puncture. He asked if you would come with him." The man looked as if he approved. "It would be good as you might help because it is an—um...unpleasant procedure."

Luke looked at Min-soo with sympathy and nodded. He shifted his gaze to Claire, who had come to stand beside him. "Lumbar puncture? Is that a spinal tap?" She nodded. "Would it be okay if I went with him?"

"Yes. I think it would be a good idea. You could be a support and a distraction. We need to make sure it's all right with the doctor, though. I know her; let's go ask."

Luke gave Min-soo a small smile and said, "Okay. Let's go, pal. We'll get this over with and maybe play some more." While the therapist was translating, Luke dropped his voice and said to Claire, "I want you to come, too. I think you're safe here, but I'd rather not have to worry about you."

Claire and Luke accompanied Min-soo and the nurse back to his room. There they met the oncologist who would be performing the procedure. The doctor shook Luke's hand and readily agreed to allow his presence. "We always prefer to give the children what they request," she said. "It can help them through the difficult times."

Min-soo was positioned on his side with his back near the edge of the bed. Claire showed Luke where to stand, near the head of the bed, with the boy facing him. A nurse stood beside the doctor and helped steady the boy while the doctor inserted a long needle between two vertebra. Skillfully, she positioned the needle and removed the stylus, allowing a small amount of clear fluid to drip into a test tube.

Luke leaned forward on the bed, holding the boy's hand and talking to him in low tones throughout the procedure. At one point, Min-soo gripped Luke's hand hard and closed his eyes tightly, but for the most part he was very still and expressionless. When the oncologist finally removed the needle, the boy sighed and let go of Luke's hand. "Thank you, sir," he whispered. He closed his eyes in obvious relief when the doctor pressed the area with a gauze pad.

"No problem." Luke gently rubbed the boy's bald head. "You did great, champ. Glad to help." Luke's voice was a little hoarse. He blinked rapidly then glanced toward Claire and asked, "What's next?"

"He'll need to lie flat for a while to try to avoid a headache." There was a slight catch in her voice when she replied, as if her own throat was tight with emotion.

"I'd like to stay with him." Luke looked at the oncologist. "Would that be all right?"

The doctor smiled and nodded. "Yes. If you can keep him still, that would be very good."

Luke turned back to Claire. "Can you bring the laptop in here to work?"

"Tell you what, I'll go get the laptop and bring in a couple of iPads." She patted Min-soo's hand. "You guys can go at it again—as long as you're still, of course." She pointed to a quiet corner. "I'll stay over there, out of your way."

Min-soo's smile was huge as he shyly eyed his new friend. "I will win."

CLAIRE AND LUKE remained at the hospital until midafternoon. During the visit, Luke was called upon several times to help hold a child or be a distraction. For the most part, he and Claire were confined to the playroom or one of the children's rooms, and other than the man early that morning, Luke didn't see anything or anyone suspicious.

After they were settled in the car ready to drive to the base, Claire leaned over and kissed Luke on the cheek. "Thank you for...well, for everything. I can't tell you how helpful it will be to have all of the data downloaded. Now I can start the analysis from your apartment." She patted the backpack that contained Luke's laptop. "Plus, well..." She fought hard to keep her tears in check. "You were terrific with the children."

He leaned across the console and returned her kiss. "It was fun." He caressed her cheek with one of his big hands and searched her eyes. "I can see why you do what you do..." He paused. Looking worried, he asked, "But what happens when things don't...when things don't work out?" He swallowed. "You said before that Min-soo was going to be okay. Why was he so pale today, and why the spinal tap?"

She couldn't resist taking his hand in both of hers. Smiling reassuringly she explained, "Min-soo started his final round of chemo yesterday, so he's experiencing fatigue and a little nausea from that. The lumbar puncture is routine, necessary to monitor his progress and to be a baseline for the chemo." She squeezed his hand. "I promise he's doing well."

Luke looked relieved and started the car. On the trip back to the base they discussed the different children, and Claire explained more about her research.

"Most of my time is spent in the playroom working with the kids, collecting data and assessing their progress. I watch them for signs of fatigue or overt illness.

"I'm getting pretty good at completing finger sticks and other blood draws while the children are busy with computer games or dogs. And, like today, when a child is too ill to come to the playroom, I'll take portable keyboards or a laptop or even a pup to them to help pass the time and treat their emotional, mental and social needs." She finished proudly. "So far, my data collection and analysis have shown that the playroom and the therapists contribute significantly to the children's recovery. I want to help start similar—um—intervention facilities in hospitals in the U.S."

"Well, I'm a believer." Luke's expression held admiration and a touch of pride. "I have every confidence that you'll make your plan a reality."

THAT EVENING, when Luke returned to the apartment for his dinner break, Claire surprised him with a home-cooked meal. He'd planned on picking her up then running to the cantina for a quick bite, so his heart did a little flutter when he entered the apartment and she came to him from the kitchen wiping her hands on a dish towel.

"Hi." Her smile was guileless and sweet. "Dinner is almost ready."

"I don't know what it is, but that smells great."

"I scoured the freezer and pantry until I was able to come up with the ingredients for spaghetti and meatballs. It's got a Minnesota twist. I hope you like it."

He grinned. "Don't care if it's Minnesota style or Midland style, I'm starved." He slipped off his jacket.

"Don't get too comfortable yet. I'd like you to do something."

"Sure. What do you need?"

She motioned to the collection of computers cluttering the dining table. "I can see that the table is rarely used for eating." She smiled at him again. "I was reluctant to move anything for fear of dislodging an important cable or messing up a connection. But unless you want to balance spaghetti on your knees in the living room, you might shove a computer aside and clear some space …"

He bent to kiss her cheek. "I would be glad to, Mary Claire." He grinned at her. "Anything for homemade spaghetti."

After dinner, Luke had to return to the surveillance compound to complete his shift, but he vowed to try to be home by ten. He was able to keep the promise and Claire waited up, greeting him when he opened the door.

They sat together on the couch, watching whatever was on the American Forces Television station and talking. After a while, Luke put his arm around Claire and pulled her closer. The embrace was comforting, and Claire curled into his warmth and soon dozed off. Sometime later he kissed her hair.

"Time for you to go to bed, sleepyhead."

Claire blinked her eyes several times and sat up. "Oh, I'm sorry. It was a really big day." She smiled shyly and added, "It was a really *good* day."

Luke couldn't admit that holding her with her head on his shoulder was one of the most wonderful half hours of his life. He pulled her to her feet and led her to the door of her bedroom. "Can I kiss you good night?" he drawled.

She didn't answer. Instead she slid her arms around his waist and tilted her head up. Standing on her toes, she lightly pressed her lips to his jaw before he leaned down and gently kissed her—once, twice and then again. "Sleep well," he whispered. "I'll see you in the morning."

CHAPTER TEN

ON SATURDAY, LUKE had to accompany a team on another reconnaissance expedition to the DMZ. When Claire woke, he was already gone. Left alone, Claire's day became tedious and lonely. She worked on her research for a while but grew tired and a little bored from her enforced confinement. Wanting to enjoy the lovely spring day, she spent several hours exploring the base. She found some places to shop and a small playground, where several mothers were watching small children on swings and slides. She passed an hour talking with them and hearing about life at Yongsan.

Luke called around five to tell her he would be late and she shouldn't wait for him for dinner. Finally, a little after ten, the door opened and he walked in. Rising from the sofa where she'd been watching a movie, Claire slipped forward to greet him. "Hi. How was your—"

Luke pulled her to his chest; his embrace seemed almost desperate. "I can't even begin to tell you how much I love you being here…" His voice was slightly hoarse.

"Luke, is everything all right?

He gave a short laugh. "Yes, it's great. I'm serious. You're here—that's almost too wonderful…" He stopped, catching himself before he went too far.

She pulled back and studied him for a moment. "You look tired. Go sit down. Can I get you something?"

"Yes, something to drink would be great." After a pause, he let her go.

"One soda coming up." She went into the kitchen and added ice to a glass, then filled it with cola. "Tell me about your day," she said as she returned to the living room.

He was slumped on the sofa, his head resting on the back cushion. "Oh, same old stuff," he mumbled.

She handed him the soft drink and then sat on the other side of the sofa facing him.

"No, seriously. Tell me what you did today. My day was really tedious and no matter what you say, I know yours wasn't. Can you give me a little vicarious action?" She pursed her lips and frowned a little.

He looked at her sympathetically. "I'm sorry you're stuck here. Not a lot to do, I know."

"I'm not pouting—well not much. Actually, my day was fine. I got to explore the base and met some really lovely women and cute kids at the park. I was able to work a lot on the research project, but… well, I just feel kind of useless." She lightly touched his hand. "But, I'd really like to hear about your day—I mean if it's okay for you to tell me."

He smiled tiredly and stroked her fingers with his thumb. "Okay, some vicarious action, then… First, one of the NCOs and I met our ride this morning about five. We drove to the Joint Security Area at Panmunjeom where we hopped in a Humvee and headed out to talk to the guards at several checkpoints across the western half of the DMZ. We check in with them periodically to verify the data they send us electronically. There have been instances when the North Koreans have successfully hacked our electronic communications so we're careful what we send via the internet, and much of the surveillance data—particularly really sensitive stuff—is reviewed in person." He took a sip of his soda. "Anyway, I spent my day being jostled in an uncomfortable jeep with four soldiers talking with their Korean counterparts."

Despite his attempt to make it sound mundane, Luke couldn't conceal his enthusiasm for his work. "Are you going to miss it?" she asked quietly.

He looked pensive. "Hmm… I guess both yes and no. I enjoy the camaraderie, and the work is interesting. And—like you said—I know it's important. What we do may mean the difference between life and death for a lot of people." He shrugged. "But I miss my family and I'm really ready to go home."

She nodded appreciatively. "Is it dangerous?"

"Uh, no… Well, not exactly." He grinned then. "Occasionally, we'll get a driver who thinks he's doing some kind of dune buggy racing and nearly tips the Humvee… And there have been helicopter patrols in bad weather—that can get a little scary. But compared to…well, never mind…" He shifted awkwardly and rubbed his neck. "I really need to get some sleep. I've been up since 4:30 and I'm beat."

She stared at him for a moment and finally leaned over and kissed his cheek. "Yes, that's a very good idea. I'm afraid you're going to pass out on the couch and I may have to carry—well, drag you to your room."

He continued to rub her arm affectionately, seeming reluctant to break contact. "Tomorrow's Sunday. Would you like to go to chapel services with me? They start about nine."

"Luke, you know I'd love that. Being a 'preacher's kid' I've always gone to church on Sunday."

He kissed her gently then, first on the mouth, just grazing her lips with his. Then he transitioned to her cheek before forcing himself to pull away. He smiled at her and said absently, "My mother's going to love you…"

Her heart did another little skipped beat, which was as much about what he'd said as in response to the gentle kisses. "Your mother?"

He grinned. "She's pretty—um—devout. Dad, too, but Mom's the one who had us all up at church two or three times a week."

Her brow creased as she tried to recall what he'd told her about his family. "Your brother… I know you said the youngest was John… The second is named…"

"Mark." He supplied. "And Matthew is the oldest."

She smiled then. Her mind flew through many of the things he had said and done for her and for others. He was unfailingly considerate and had always been a gentleman with her. He was patient and protective. He hadn't pushed her or made any physical demands.

She kissed his cheek. "You know, I think I'm going to like your mother, too."

WHEN CLAIRE EMERGED from the bedroom the next morning, she smelled the mingled aromas of maple syrup, waffles and coffee. Amazingly, Luke was in the kitchen cooking breakfast. She'd rarely seen him wearing anything other than his uniform or the camouflage he wore for the times he was on patrol in the north. This morning he was neatly dressed in tan slacks and a white cotton shirt. She stared for a moment to where the long sleeves were rolled back revealing his strong forearms.

He was engrossed in rinsing blueberries and didn't see her. "Hey," she said, "that smells great. I had no idea you could cook."

Caught off guard, his head flew up and his eyes pinned her. Somewhat self-consciously Claire adjusted the skirt of her light-weight, flowing, flowery dress, which reached a few inches past her knees. Her hair was loose and straight, falling almost to the middle of her back.

"What can I say? I'm just a regular renaissance man." His strong accent and slightly "off" pronunciation of the word made her giggle. He grinned. "You're just in time to set the table. I've already pushed back the computers."

They laughed a lot over breakfast as he told her more stories about growing up with three really rough brothers. "My grandparents—Mom's family—owned a cotton farm in the north part of the Permian Basin. When Mom couldn't control us any longer—which was quite a lot of the time—she sent us to stay with them—in various numbers and arrangements. Believe it or not, I was one of the best behaved—being a middle child and all. But I still spent a lot of time banished to Andrews. Anyway, we grew up riding tractors, pulling plows and driving beat-up pickups."

"Did you fight a lot?"

"Oh, yeah. We were forever on top of one another, or rolling around with fists pounding. But we always stopped short of hurting each other. Now, of course, we're all best friends."

After breakfast Claire washed the dishes while Luke finished getting ready. A short time later he emerged from his room carrying a guitar case. Before she could comment, he gave a wry grin. "When I'm here, I help out with the music."

She appeared a little taken aback. "I don't know why I'm surprised. I guess you just seem the football type, not really the musical type."

"I told you," he said, "I'm a renaissance man. The musical abilities come from the Llewellyn side of the family. Dad's relatives were very musical, and he made sure we all learned to play something. Matt and Ruthie play the piano, Mark is a drummer and passable violin player, then Johnny and I play guitar. Most everyone is above average singing—well, my brother John is the exception—he's totally tone deaf."

THEY WALKED SEVERAL blocks to the large building that housed Yongsan's chapel. While waiting for the service to start, Luke introduced Claire to several friends and colleagues. They were talking to a young Army officer who worked on Luke's team when a stylishly dressed, attractive red-head approached. Luke broke off the conversation and gave the newcomer a quick hug. Claire couldn't contain a twinge of jealously as she watched the ease and affection between the pair.

"Hi, gorgeous. I haven't seen you in a while. Have you heard from Littlejohn?" Luke asked.

"Yes," she said, beaming. "I talked to him yesterday. He thinks he'll be back sometime at the end of the week." Her lively green eyes and wide smile were engaging.

Luke nodded. "Kind of what I thought." He turned to Claire and said, "Claire, let me introduce you to someone you need to meet. This is Bridgette McDonald. She's a nurse at the base hospital doing something in the E.R. I'm sure she can tell you all about it. Bridgette, this is Claire Olsen. I mentioned her to you last week."

Bridgette grinned knowingly. "Ah. That's what I thought. It's great to meet you, Claire. Luke was kind of obnoxious when I talked with him last. He told me all about this nurse he'd met—"

"Hey," Luke interrupted, looking embarrassed. "That was not meant to be repeated!"

Bridgette wrinkled her nose at Luke and smiled conspiringly to Claire. "I'll tell you later." Luke scowled at her but then shook his head and sighed good-naturedly.

Despite her initial hint of concern over Luke's easy relationship with the attractive young woman, Claire felt a quick affinity toward the other nurse. "Hi, Bridgette. It's nice to meet you. I'll be sure and ask later what all Luke said…" She peered at Luke and was rewarded when he gave her hand a quick squeeze.

"Okay, fine. You two talk it out. I can't stop you." With a pained look, he pointed to a row of chairs near the stage. "Have a seat. I need to head up to the front now. I'll join you after the singing." He gave her a wink and smile, then left carrying his guitar.

When they were alone, Bridgette and Claire took their seats, leaving the aisle spot for Luke. "Are you in the Army?" Claire asked.

"No, I'm a civilian. I've been here off and on for about five years. Long story."

"How well do you know Luke?" Claire couldn't keep the question inside.

Bridgette answered very matter-of-factly. "Oh pretty well. We've been together quite a lot." Her eyebrows lifted and her voice was cheerful. "I normally spend a considerable amount of time at the apartment."

"Oh. All right." Claire blinked.

Claire's disappointment and trace of jealously must have been evident, because Bridgette gave a short laugh and hastened to add, "No, wait, don't get the wrong impression. I don't go to the apartment to see Luke. I go to see Brad." She smiled brightly and held up her left hand. "We're engaged."

Claire's relief was obvious when she smiled back. Obligingly, she took Bridgette's fingers to admire her ring. "Oh, I see." She grinned and rolled her eyes a little. "I'm sorry, you kind of took me by surprise." She thought a minute and then looked puzzled. "But when we first saw you, Luke asked if you'd talked to John. Who is John?"

It was Bridgette's turn to be confused. She shook her head. "No, he just asked me about Brad."

"Yes, I'm sure of it. I think he actually called him '*Little* John.' I wasn't sure if he was just teasing or being condescending. I mean pretty much everyone is 'little' to Luke."

"Hah!" Bridgette laughed. "That's pretty funny. That's his name!" Claire still looked baffled. "Brad's last name is 'Littlejohn'. All one word." She gave a small sigh. "I'm going to have to live with it, too. 'Bridgette Littlejohn'…"

Claire nodded then glanced up to the stage where Luke was talking with another guitar player. "This is all really new to me. It's happened so fast and I'm still not sure…about our relationship…" She sighed. "Plus, there's a lot going on right now."

"I think I understand. Luke told us about you right after he met you last weekend." She smiled. "He came home from his embassy gig practically talking our ears off about a terrific girl he'd met. I've known Luke for about a year and that was the first time either Brad or I have heard him talk like that." She smiled proudly. "Of course, we encouraged him—well, badgered, actually—to ask you out. I think you have

Brad and me to thank for giving him the nerve to actually do it!"

The women were still chuckling when the music started. The audience was instructed to rise and the service began.

For the first time since coming to Korea, Claire felt comfortable in her surroundings. Most of those present in the chapel were American. The songs were familiar and the atmosphere reminded her of going to church at home. She hadn't realized before that she'd been a little homesick.

Luke was one of five people on the stage leading the singing. In addition to him, there were two other guitarists, a drummer and a woman playing an electronic keyboard. All were competent musicians and they sounded good together. It was fun, entertaining and oddly enlightening to watch and listen to Luke. Several times he glanced at her and smiled, giving her a warm feeling and causing her heart to skip a beat.

AFTER THE CHAPEL service, Claire and Luke had lunch at the Officers' Club. They asked Bridgette to join them, but she declined, citing the need to get ready for work. She winked at Claire, though, and Claire guessed that her excuse was contrived. She smiled at her new friend and winked back.

As they were leaving the club, Luke glanced at Claire's feet. "Are those shoes comfortable?"

Claire looked down at her ballet flats and then back up at Luke. Puzzled by the question, she replied, "Yes. They're quite comfortable. Why?"

"I mean can you walk in them for a while? Like several miles."

"Yes, I guess. Why?"

"I have a treat for you. Something you're going to love." He grabbed her hand and pulled her toward the nearest gate. "Come on. We need to find a cab."

TWENTY MINUTES LATER they emerged from a taxi at the entrance to Seoul's equivalent of Central Park. Claire had seen the small mountain that marked the center of the city from a distance, and was familiar with the tall tower that graced its peak. The area was comprised of rolling, wooded hills, complete with numerous trails and wide walking paths.

"This is Namsan Park," Luke explained. He took her hand and followed a group of people moving toward one of the wide paths. "There's actually a cable car that goes to the top, but I think you'll like this better."

After being largely confined to the base for several days, and with much of that time spent in the apartment, Claire rejoiced at the opportunity to be outside, walking in a park on a lovely April afternoon.

"So where are we going?" she asked.

"Up."

"Okay. I'm game. What are we going to see?"

"Just wait. It won't take long."

True to Luke's prediction, they had walked only a few hundred yards, moving steadily up the path toward the top of the hill, when they made a turn. Before them was a magnificent display of flowering trees, covered with small white blossoms. The trees lined both sides of the wide path, trailing up the mountain until the path turned again, out of sight, but continuing upward. At many places the trees met overhead, creating a canopy.

Claire gasped at the lovely sight. "Oh, my gosh! It's beautiful. What are they?"

"Cherry blossoms." Luke's answer was barely above a whisper. He was not looking at the flowering trees, rather, he was watching her.

Claire felt like a child at Christmas. They wound their way up the mountain and with each turn in the path, she exclaimed again at the beauty before them. She didn't mind that the park was crowded with others who'd come to enjoy the annual sight. It was as if they were the only couple on the lovely mountain set in the vast city.

Hand in hand they strolled for nearly an hour, slowly making their way along the trail shaded by the white blooming trees. When they arrived at the top of the mountain, they came to a large landing area, probably at least a quarter mile square. At the crest was the base of the Seoul Tower, which rose nearly 800 feet above them.

"Want to go up?" Luke asked as Claire

squinted to look at the top of the steel-and-concrete structure.

She looked at the long line of people waiting for the elevator and shook her head. "No, not really. If it's okay with you, I'd rather just stay here in the park and enjoy the flowers."

They walked a little farther down the back side of the mountain, looking for a spot that was a bit less crowded. Finally, they located a deserted bench and sat down. Luke stretched out his legs, leaned his head back and closed his eyes, seeming to enjoy the warmth of the sun on his face.

Claire sat back on the bench and observed the passersby. There were many young couples, clearly courting, much like her and Luke. She stared in awe when she observed that many of the young women were wearing very short skirts and very high heels. Marveling at the challenge of maneuvering the fairly steep path in three-inch heels, she said, "I'm afraid I would trip and fall trying to go downhill on those shoes!"

Luke laughed. "I have to say that it's impressive, and I would imagine pretty painful. That's why I asked if yours were comfortable."

She giggled. "And I appreciate it!"

They watched the park's visitors a little more. Young couples were pushing baby strollers and carrying small children. They saw older couples strolling by and even the occasional group of tourists. A slight breeze ruffled her hair, and Claire saw hundreds of small white petals rain down on the path.

"What are you thinking?" Luke's voice was quiet, and he was studying her.

"That you were so right. This has been one of my favorite days ever." She shyly clasped his hand. "Thank you for bringing me."

He laced his fingers with hers. "My pleasure."

They sat a few more minutes enjoying the people and the showering petals. After a while, Luke broke the silence. "I have a question. Just checking—to be sure… Ahem…"

Claire turned her attention from the people and flowers to the man. "Luke, what?"

"I need to clarify something." He shifted

nervously. "You're not involved with any-one back in Minnesota, are you?"

Claire pulled her hand away and frowned. Her voice carried an edge when she answered. "Luke, if I was 'involved' with someone at home, I wouldn't be here with you." Her jaw tensed.

Luke swallowed and looked up toward the lovely blue sky before turning back to her. "I'm sorry, I didn't mean any offense. Don't be upset, I just needed to be sure." He took her hand again. "It's important to me."

Her brief spot of anger evaporated, and she sighed. "Luke, I've never been involved with anyone, period. I really haven't dated much. Because of being home-schooled and my time spent skating, I wasn't around boys other than my church youth groups. And then when I started college, I was pretty immature, relatively speaking, and I'm…well, kind of on the shy side…" She shrugged and looked down at nothing in particular. "Since then, I've mostly focused on school and work, and no one has been interested enough…"

"Are the men in Minnesota stupid or something?"

Her only response was a rueful half smile. They were quiet again for a few minutes.

Something suddenly occurred to Claire. "Are you?" She gnawed on her lip and searched Luke's face. "Are you involved with anyone?"

His eyes held hers. "No, I'm not." He looked away then, his gaze drifting to his hands. "Not now." A minute passed and she was quiet, waiting for him to continue. "I was engaged once." He was still addressing his hands. "Her name was Whitney. She was one of my sister's roommates in college. We met when I was a junior at Annapolis. She was—er, she is—blonde, bubbly and gregarious." He finally looked at her again. "I fell head over heels.

"At Christmas during my senior year, I was home on leave and asked her to marry me... I was thrilled when she agreed and we set the date for July after I graduated. That spring, she told me she wanted to put off the wedding for a year, until after my first deployment. That way she could graduate and then join me wherever I was stationed. That made sense, so I left for the Persian Gulf. I was young, only 21, but I was also very much in love with her."

Luke was watching Claire carefully and saw the flash of pain in her expression when he said that. He gently rubbed her fingers with his thumb. "Claire, I want you to know." She nodded and he continued. "Anyway, I was gone for just under eleven months. I kept her picture with me all the time. We were at sea and often in blackout situations, but I wrote and emailed whenever I could. She wrote less often, but I rationalized that she was busy. We would Skype pretty regularly. As time went on, I could tell that she was cooling toward me. The letters and calls became less and less frequent. I didn't want to admit what was happening… Anyway, to make a long, very common story short, when I got back, I immediately went to see her—even before I went home."

His voice became remorseful. "Imagine my surprise… When she saw me she started crying and told me that she was getting married to someone else. She was four months pregnant."

' His gaze shifted to the cherry blossoms above. "We had never—er—had sex. She told me—well, we both thought we should wait until after we were married." His eyes finally found hers again. "Obviously, she felt differently about the other guy."

"Obviously, she was an idiot." Claire couldn't hide the unexpected surge of jealousy.

Her irritable comment surprised a chuckle out of Luke. He squeezed her hand. "That's pretty much it, except to say that I was devastated. It took me a couple of years to get over... Well, anyway, I haven't dated much since then." He gave her a wry look. "Mostly because of lack of opportunity, but also, I guess because I have 'trust issues'."

"So, what did your family say? I know it doesn't help when you're hurting that much, but I bet they were very supportive."

"Actually, Ruthie told me she was really glad about—well, about how it had worked out. She called Whitney 'high maintenance,' and said she wasn't nearly good enough for me. It was a very sweet thing to say, but Ruthie is very loyal to the family. And I know my mom in particular was overjoyed. She told me that it was for the best. She said she always believed that Whitney was more interested in my money than me." He rolled his eyes and shook his head.

"Well, it sounds like Ruthie was right. She wasn't good enough for you. Plus, *I'm* right, she was *stupid!*"

He laughed and kissed her nose. "I think you're wonderful." He stood. "Well, enough about that. It was way in the past, but it's something I didn't want to keep from you. It's starting to get dark, Ms. Olsen. We probably need to be heading down the mountain."

She smiled at him and held his hand as they strolled among the cherry blossoms.

They were quiet for a while, both lost in their thoughts. As they turned the last corner near the bottom of the mountain she glanced at him and asked, "Your mom thought Whitney was after your money? I didn't know naval officers made that much." She thought about that a moment before adding, "Of course, they must make more than oncology nurses…"

His brow creased briefly, then he responded, "We do all right." He smiled sheepishly. "But there are a lot of benefits. For example, you get to meet beautiful young women who've had their passports stolen."

"Oh." She returned his smile. "I guess there are benefits."

CHAPTER ELEVEN

THAT EVENING AFTER DINNER, Luke was working at the dining table. He moved from a computer to a laptop, splitting his attention between the screens and moving his hands from one keyboard to the other. Although Claire didn't say anything, he sensed her presence and looked up.

In that first nanosecond, all thoughts were erased from Luke's mind and he could think of absolutely nothing but her. She had showered and gotten ready for bed. Her shiny black hair was lying across her shoulders and down her back. She was wearing an oversized Green Bay Packers jersey, which reached almost to her knees, and she was barefoot. His mouth was suddenly dry and his heart started beating irregularly. Not fully conscious of what he was doing, he stood.

It was instinct, not experience, that allowed

Claire to recognize Luke's reaction —desire. She swallowed hard, instantly uncertain. She knew she needed to do something—say something—but was at a loss. Her heart was thudding painfully and she bit her lip as she tried to gauge his thoughts and anticipate his actions.

Luke could barely breathe. He recognized the sensation—during his football days he'd had the wind knocked out of him on more than one occasion. The constriction in his chest at that instant rivaled the feeling caused by a blow from a 300-pound defensive lineman. He knew he was staring, but nothing short of an earthquake could tear his eyes from her.

He was so attuned to Claire he could see that she was struggling with apprehension that might border on fright. He knew he needed to react—to say something, anything, to break the tension. After a couple of deep breaths, inspiration hit.

"The Packers? *Seriously?*"

The tension shattered.

She glanced down at the jersey. "Yeah. So?" One corner of her mouth turned up. "You have a problem with cheeseheads?"

"*Please*… Like there's any football team except the Cowboys?" He motioned to the front door. "That's it. You have to leave now. I can't share an apartment with a Green Bay fan." He took two steps in her direction. "Here, I'll help you pack."

She giggled and shook her head. "The Cowboys? I should have known. You guys from Texas are *so* predictable. You need to stretch, consider other possibilities. Jerry Jones and company are not the only game in town."

"Yeah, but the Packers?" He sighed. "I would have thought at least the Vikings."

"Can't help it. It's a family thing." She held out her hands in mock resignation. "I can see we're at an impasse. It looks like we're going to have to come to some sort of compromise…"

He shook his head doubtfully. "I don't know…I have to consider the full implications. If my grandfather found out, I could be disowned."

"Hmm…I may have to remember that for future blackmailing attempts."

"Okay, I guess I'll let you stay for now."

He chuckled. "But we'd better wait till later to discuss baseball loyalties."

Claire smiled and stepped closer, and Luke saw that she was holding something.

"I was wondering if you could help me. It should only take a few minutes." Once again, she seemed a little hesitant.

"Sure. What is it?"

"I need to take out my stitches. They've been in over a week and should go. I can't do it myself, because it's my right arm, and I'm just not that coordinated. And, I don't want to have to go somewhere to have it done."

Luke crossed the short distance that still separated them. "Here, let me take a look." He raised her arm and for the first time actually saw the result of the knife attack. As he'd been told, the wound was long, running almost the full length of the underside of her right forearm. His examination revealed more than two dozen small black stitches that were closely spaced, neatly mending the long, slightly curving cut. The doctor who had sutured the laceration had done a very nice job; the wound itself was well on its way to being healed.

Luke lightly ran his forefinger along the stitches. He nodded and said, "It might hurt a little."

"It's all right." She met his stare for a moment and swallowed hard. "I'm tougher than I look." She lifted her other hand, which contained a wash cloth, a pair of tweezers and a pair of manicure scissors. "I've disinfected the forceps and scissors, so I think everything's ready to go."

Luke pulled two chairs away from the table, angling them to get the best light. He sat directly across from her, with their knees touching. She looked at him with a hint of confusion when he picked up the tweezers and scissors, which looked tiny in his large hands. "To be honest, you surprised me, Luke. Most lay people are really hesitant about things like this. I thought I'd have to coax you into taking them out."

"Please," he scoffed as he deftly picked up the knot of the first suture with the tweezers. "I've had this done *to* me so many times, I could probably *do* the stitching." He looked up and grinned. "Now mind you, my attempts wouldn't look nearly this nice…"

With no fuss and very minimal discomfort, Luke snipped, pulled and disposed of the tiny stitches. When he'd removed the last one, he set the miniature scissors and tweezers on the table and once again lightly rubbed the length of the reddened scar with his finger. Leaning forward, he pressed his lips to it soothingly. "Mom always said that'll make it better," he murmured. He raised his gaze again to watch her.

Claire's breath caught and she stiffened. The tension between them returned in a flash. "Umm, thanks. I don't think Dr. Kim could have done a better job." She gave him a weak smile.

Trying to avoid his scrutiny, Claire gestured toward the computers. "What were you working on? Something to do with surveillance? More boats with too many people?" She spoke a little too quickly.

His eyes remained on her face for a moment longer. Finally he tore them away and shook his head in response. "No." He pointed to two laptops and a separate desktop tower and monitor. "Those computers are actually my personal ones. I was working on something for my dad and brothers." He motioned to another computer tower connected to two monitors. The screens were dark, although tiny green blinking lights indicated that they were "on". "Those are the work computers."

"Oh. So what are you working on for your family?"

"Actually," he said, "I'm just helping out a little with a project... From time to time they send me stuff to analyze... You know, beyond Packers and Cowboys, we probably need to talk about some other—um—important things where we may have some differences of opinion."

"What kinds of things?"

His lips thinned. "Uh...well, for example, are you a super environmentalist or anything?"

She sat back, a bit surprised by the question. "No, not particularly. Of course, I'm concerned about clean air and water and not littering and all... I guess I'm about average. Why do you ask?"

"How do you feel about global warming?"

She actually giggled. "Luke, I'm from

Minnesota. Ask any Minnesotan in any given February and we're pretty much in agreement that we'd appreciate a little global warming."

His relief showed. "Ah, well, what about hydraulic fracturing?"

"Hydraulic fracturing?" She looked puzzled. "You mean fracking? Like oil drilling? I guess I never thought about it. Why?"

"Oh, nothing." He decided to change the subject. Pointing to her oversized jersey, he said, "Okay, your turn. Tell me about the Packers and family loyalty."

Willing to be distracted, she smiled. "Oh, that comes from Mom's side of the family. She was born and raised in Oshkosh, Wisconsin. Her father and his brothers were an early part of the Green Bay consortium that owns the Packers. It just kind of persisted from there."

He frowned. "Your mother was born in Wisconsin?" Luke kept his voice quiet and expressionless.

"Well, yes. Born and raised there, along with two sisters, by George and Maribel Appleton." She blinked at his suddenly subdued manner, but continued. "My Grammy was a huge Bart Starr fan…" Claire tried another smile. "Luke, is something wrong?"

"Your mother isn't Asian?" His tone was flat.

Claire shook her head. "No. She's mostly Norwegian, I think. Maybe some Irish… Why do you ask?" Her eyes suddenly got wider and her lips thinned. "You assumed she was Asian, because of how I look." Claire blinked and seemed to withdraw. "Obviously, I was adopted. Does that matter?"

HE DIDN'T ANSWER immediately. Luke stared at her and then through her.

"You were adopted," he repeated. His mouth tensed and a furrow appeared between his brows. He turned his stare to the computers. "Adopted." The word was an echo. "*Stupid!*" he hissed under his breath, shaking his head angrily. "I can't believe I missed that."

Claire was crushed. She stood and paced a few steps away. "My parents are the greatest," she murmured. "For some reason they couldn't have children. They didn't have a lot of money… It took years…" She realized she was crying. Why was he making an issue out of something that was precious to her? Sniffing, she picked up the washcloth to wipe her eyes. At that moment, she was acutely disappointed in Luke—apparently her adoption was a problem to him. Evidently he didn't like it or approve of it. Her disillusionment was profound; he was not the man she believed him to be.

Her sniff seemed to get Luke's attention, and his eyes shifted from one of the computers to hers. She read anger and looked quickly away. Her words were subdued. "I'm sorry if that bothers you." She wiped her eyes again. "I think I'll go to bed—"

CLAIRE'S TEARS AND DISTRESS finally cut through Luke's silent deliberation, and his splintered attention crashed back to the room. He quickly rose and caught her hand, halting her exit and pulling her back to sit across from him. "Wait… Wait… Just a minute." He stared at her. "I'm still trying to get it… You're Korean, then? You were adopted from here?" It was as much a statement as a question. He was trying to work out this puzzle.

"Yes, I was adopted from here! But what difference does that make? So what?" Her voice rose and the tears were coming more quickly. "It's neither good nor bad—it just is! And I don't understand why it would matter to you?"

Luke finally understood. Searching her face, he saw the heartbreak in her eyes. He stood and pulled her into his arms. "Oh, Mary Claire, no." His tone softened and became soothing once more. "I'm sorry I gave the wrong impression. Please don't cry!" He hugged her tightly and muttered, "Honey, I don't care if you came from Minnesota or Korea or Texas or Klingon. It doesn't matter to me a whit that you were adopted. The only thing that matters is you, period." He tenderly wiped her tears with his thumbs and gazed into her startlingly lovely eyes. "Mary Claire, I'm in love with you."

She studied his face for a breath then whispered, "Please say that again."

He grinned. "The 'Please don't cry' part

or the 'I don't care if you're from Klingon' part?"

She gave a watery giggle and punched him in the shoulder. "The 'I'm in love with you' part."

"I love you." He pulled her head onto his shoulder and cradled it with his big hands. His voice was soft. "I think you already know that I love you, and have pretty much since I watched the video of you fighting back when those guys tried to kill you." His arms tightened around her. He turned his face and kissed her hair then gently lifted her chin to touch her lips in a soft, sweet kiss.

"Your turn," he said, hoping Claire couldn't detect the insecurity in his voice. "I need you to tell me. How do you feel?"

She didn't hesitate. "I love you." She bit her lip and then continued. "I probably have since you said 'please' when you asked me out the first time... Or maybe even before that... It might have been when you called Jessica 'Miss Olsen.' I didn't understand it then, but I wanted you to notice me, and I was disappointed when you didn't." She swallowed hard and added, "That's why I was so hurt and disillusioned just now when I thought that you disapproved of me being adopted."

He laughed and there was a release in the sound. "Okay, well, there you go. I did notice and—wow—I've never felt this good or been this happy." He kissed her again and picked her up, swinging her in a quick, joyful circle. "It seems weird to be grateful that you were the victim of a knife attack, but I'm glad for whatever it took to make our paths cross."

He kissed her again and ran his hands through her hair. Finally, he let go and said, "I hate to be a buzzkill, but we need to talk." He took her hand and led her back to the sofa, pulling her down beside him.

He searched her eyes, serious once more. "You're Korean. You were born here." It was important to verify the fact.

"Yes, Luke. I was born here. My parents adopted me through an agency in Seattle. I was taken to the U.S. when I was about six months old. Of course, I don't recall any of that… I've not been back until a month ago."

"What do you know about it?"

"Not a whole lot. I was told that up until eight or ten years ago, Korean adoptions to the U.S. were quite common. They're considerably rarer now, because the Korean government is trying to promote local adoptions since Koreans are having too few children."

"Who knows about it?"

"Why, pretty much everyone I know. Certainly everyone I grew up with." She gave a tiny shrug. "Luke, it's obvious."

"No. That's not what I meant, Claire. Who knows here?"

Claire sat up straighter and stared at him. She bit her lip and whispered, "You think that's it, don't you?" She looked stricken.

"Who knows here?" His tone was brusque, and he emphasized each word.

Her mouth opened and closed before she was able to answer. "The second week I was in Seoul, I went to the orphanage." She took a breath. "It's called the Asian Social Welfare Agency. It's an adoption agency, located not all that far from Youngsai Women's College and Seoul National University."

"Who did you talk to?"

"One of the assistant directors—a Mrs. Lee."

"What did she tell you?"

"Not all that much, really. I showed her my paperwork—what my parents had been given when I was adopted—"

"Do you have the papers here?" he interrupted.

"Yes. I didn't want to leave them at Jessica's, so I brought them with me. I can show you." She started to get up, but he stopped her.

"Later. Tell me first." He kept his arm around her, reluctant to let her leave. Unable to resist, he kissed her lightly on the lips. "This is getting much too natural." His voice was a little rough. He cleared his throat and pulled away. "Okay, go on."

Her smile was lovely, and he longed to kiss her again, but he knew this was too important.

"So, I showed Mrs. Lee the paperwork and talked to her for about fifteen minutes. She spoke English pretty well, probably about like the detective yesterday. I answered some questions, filled out a form

with my contact information and signed
a release document. Anyway, she left for
a few minutes and came back with a file.
It was in Korean, of course, but she said
that she had my birth mother's name and
address, and also information about my
foster mother—the woman who cared for
me before I was sent to Minnesota. The information hadn't been updated since I was
born. Mrs. Lee said she would send a letter
to my birth mother asking if she wanted
to meet me. She assured me that this is
all standard and about half of the time the
birth mothers want to meet the adoptees,
but half the time they don't. She said she
would contact me when she heard back."

Claire shrugged. "She hasn't called
yet. I haven't really thought much of it.
I would like to meet my birth mother, of
course, and learn what I can about her."
She paused and studied his eyes. "That's
one of the reasons I wanted to be assigned
to this particular research project. When
Cindy Sung—my mentor—proposed the
opportunity, I jumped at the chance... I'd
also like to learn about my father." She
shifted a little. "Clearly he wasn't Korean.

The agency didn't have a name or any information about him."

Neither spoke for a moment, both deep in thought. Finally Claire repeated her earlier question. "You think that's it, don't you?" Worry etched her face. "For some reason, someone doesn't want me to be here."

"Claire, I'm not concerned that someone doesn't want you to be here. It's that they don't want you to be *alive.* I told you, they were trying to *kill* you!" He rubbed his eyes. "Did Mrs. Lee give you anything? Any papers we could use to learn more?"

"No, not really. She gave me copies of the form I filled out and the release form. I have them with the other papers my parents gave me. Do you want to see them now?" He nodded and she left the room for a moment to fetch the papers.

When she returned Luke had moved from the sofa to the dining table and logged on to one of his personal computers. She handed the papers to him and he scanned them. While she watched, he pulled up the website of the Asian Social

Welfare Agency. Without talking to Claire, took out his cell phone and placed a call.

"Henry," he said. "Yeah, it's Luke. I need some help finding out about a Korean adoption that happened 25 years ago…No, it's personal…Yeah, I've got a little. Here, I'm emailing you the basic information now." She watched as his fingers sped across the keyboard. "Okay, I sent you the links and the old case number, a birth date, and a number from a new release form…Yeah, you got it?…Good…See what you can find from the Korean databases and email it to me…No problem, I understand…Great, thanks." He clicked off.

Luke typed a few more keys and then looked up at Claire. "That was Henry Kim, one of our local informants. He's a computer geek like me, but from the Korean side. If there's anything to be found in cyberspace about your adoption, he'll find it. He told me it might take a few days, though, depending on how deep he has to go into public records… That is, assuming there are public records. We'll give him a couple of days and maybe go back to the adoption agency to talk with Mrs. Lee again."

Her mouth tensed and she looked anxious. "Why would it matter to anyone that I came to Korea and tried to locate my birth mother?"

He shrugged. "Who knows? I can only speculate. But here's an idea. You could ask Jessica. She might have some insight. Does she know you were born here?'

"No, we never talked about it. I guess it would have made sense to mention it, but I've always felt it was private"

"It's just a thought. Since she's something of an expert on Korean culture—"

Luke's comment was interrupted by his cell phone. Glancing at the caller ID, he pressed his lips together and swore under his breath. His irritation wasn't evident, however, when he pressed the button to answer. "Llewellyn."

CLAIRE WATCHED Luke's changing expressions as he listened to the caller and occasionally responded with curt acknowledgments. During the mostly one-sided conversation, she read impatience, frustration, skepticism, curiosity and finally, resignation. After about a minute, he turned to the two darkened computers and hit a series of keys on each; immediately they responded with faint whirring sounds and came to life.

"Okay, Jack, I'm pulling up the images." More keys were struck and a black-and-white satellite photo was displayed on one screen. Concurrently, the second screen held multiple columns of numbers interspersed with letters, indicative of some sort of code. Luke clicked the mouse several times to zoom in on one spot of the satellite image. "Yeah, I see it. It could be a Nodong or even a Taepodong." He studied the screen holding the columns of codes and frowned as he listened for a brief time. "No, I really doubt it's a Taepodong 2, but we need to be sure… Yeah, I know. See what you can do to get more accurate measurements and keep the line to ROK Command open." He glanced at his watch and mumbled, "I'll be there in five." He clicked off the phone and frowned again at the satellite image before signing off on both computers.

Finally, his eyes moved to capture Claire's. Shaking his head, he sighed and said, "I've gotta go."

"Something serious?" she asked.

Luke rose and crossed the two steps to reach her. Rubbing her cheek lightly, he answered, "Maybe yes, but probably not. It looks like the North Koreans are moving a missile. They do that from time to time, just to remind us they have them. They've repeatedly threatened to use them. You know, old standbys like 'we will rain down a sea of fire' or 'we will turn Seoul to ashes'—blah, blah, blah, blah." He grinned and wagged his head a little from side to side. Then, his mouth tightened. "But when they move them at night—like now—we get a little nervous. I need to go check it out." He smiled reassuringly and leaned down to kiss her cheek before heading toward his bedroom.

In seconds he returned with his jacket and moved to the front door. "This will likely take several hours, so don't wait up." He looked at her with yearning. Finally, with a frustrated half smile, he waved. "See you in the morning."

It was just after ten when Luke left the apartment. Claire spent the next hour talking to her parents and then reading. About eleven she was having trouble keeping her eyes open and decided to go to bed. She hadn't been alone in the apartment at night and wasn't sure whether to leave a light on for Luke's return. After a brief moment of consideration, she turned on the living room lamp and retired.

She was asleep in minutes. Her thoughts swirled happily, recalling the look on Luke's face when he'd declared his love.

CHAPTER TWELVE

THERE WAS A NOISE.

Claire roused from a deep sleep and tried to determine what had awakened her. Still confused and a little disoriented, she raised her head and listened for a few seconds, but there was only silence. She was about to conclude that there had been no sound when it happened again—a deep, eerie, guttural moan that was only barely human. Instantaneously, her heart was pounding painfully. She held her breath as she sat up and listened.

"No, no! *Stop! Get back!*" The words were hushed, muffled by the closed door, but she immediately recognized Luke's voice. Scrambling out of bed, she fumbled around for the lamp switch and sat for only a second, trying to think—knowing she needed to act.

A weapon—she needed a weapon. She

glanced around the room, searching for something to use, then she remembered she'd seen a couple of baseball bats—probably Brad's—in the closet when she'd put away her clothes.

Claire rushed to the closet, grabbed an aluminum bat and without hesitation threw open her bedroom door and peered into the living room. Nothing appeared to be disturbed, but she noted that the lamp had been turned off. Cautiously, she turned it back on and glanced around; nothing seemed to be out of the ordinary.

Another moan and a shout came from Luke's room and she lifted the bat to her shoulder and sped across to his closed door, pausing only briefly to listen. The sounds were faint, but she heard someone thrashing wildly. Trying to be quiet, she turned the knob, raising the bat over her head, and ran in.

"Halt! Don't move!" Claire skidded to a stop at the hoarse command. The light from the lamp reached past the doorway. Quickly, she scanned the dark room, trying to identify the source of the threat to Luke. She had expected to see him in a physical

fight with an intruder, but she was stunned to see that he was alone. Despite the darkness, she could tell that he was half sitting, half kneeling in the middle of his bed. The bedclothes were in disarray and had been thrown aside. Luke's eyes were open, but he appeared to be looking in the direction of the window, away from her.

She took a step forward, moving more completely into the room. Her breath was rapid but shallow, and her heart was beating erratically. "Luke," she whispered.

Luke seemed to lurch forward on the bed, almost falling face down before bracing himself on his hands, then springing back up to his knees.

"Watch out!" His scream was hoarse. His eyes, although open, were unseeing— or rather, they were focused on something that wasn't there.

A nightmare. It was only a nightmare. Relief flooded through Claire and she was able to steady her breathing a bit. Realizing there was no external threat gave her new-found confidence, and she set the bat down on the floor then slipped a little closer to the bed. She briefly debated whether or not to wake him, but then he moaned again and jerked to one side, and she became concerned that he might injure himself. She eased forward and approached him cautiously. He was now facing away from her and she held out her hand to touch him lightly on his right shoulder. She tried to keep her voice steady as she quietly said, "Luke, wake—"

He cried out again. "*No! Get back!*" Then he swung his massive arm back, away from his body, slamming her across the chest. A harsh gasp was forced from her as he hit her squarely, sending her reeling across the room.

Claire actually became airborne, flying a few inches off the ground before landing on her side and skidding. Her slide was halted when she hit the door jamb hard with her shoulder. A cry escaped her lips and she came to a stop, stunned, on the far side of the room.

LUKE WAS SUDDENLY AWARE, but he was very disoriented. Seconds passed. He realized he was kneeling in his bed. His entire body was wet—almost as if he'd just gotten out of the shower. He had hit someone; he could still feel the vestige of the contact on the back of his right forearm. He knew there had been two cries. That was what had awakened him—either the contact or the sound of the muffled cries. His heart thundered in his chest and he was breathing hard, as though he'd just sprinted a mile. More seconds passed as he shook his head, trying to clear it.

Then he heard a sound—like a faint sigh. With crushing apprehension, he turned toward the sound, and in the dim light from the open doorway, he saw her. She was curled next to the wall by his bedroom door, crumpled like a little doll. Her eyes were huge as she stared at him.

"Dear God, no." His harsh words were quiet now but at least as mournful as before. "No, please, no!" He scrambled to his feet, nearly overwhelmed by a wave of nausea as he rushed to where she was lying. "Claire...Claire, please..."

She cringed when he reached out to her. He knelt beside her. His touch was gentle as he placed both hands on her upper arms, trying to help her sit up. "Oh, please, no," he repeated. "Honey, are you hurt?" His accent was stronger than usual, and the words were plaintive. "Please, tell me if I hurt you." He ran his hands across her upper arms and back, searching for evidence of injury and fervently praying he would find none.

"Luke, I'm okay. It's okay." Seeing that he was alert again relieved Claire enormously, and she was able to focus briefly on herself. She would no doubt have bruises on her hip and shoulder, but she hadn't hit her head and knew from years of experience falling repeatedly on the ice that she was not seriously injured. "You didn't hurt me, Luke. I'm okay." She repeated the reassurances several times, hoping to convince and trying to console.

Finally, he accepted that she was, indeed, all right. The look on his face changed from terror to shame, remorse and a different kind of fear. He rose slowly and moved stiffly away from her.

As Claire studied him, she detected that a barrier or curtain seemed to crash down, separating them. That was when she became aware that he was only wearing raggedy gym shorts. Although his size and strength were obvious to anyone who came in contact with him, it was the first time she'd actually seen his heavily muscled chest and arms. She swallowed and stared. The raw power evident by his size and bulk was truly fearsome.

Still a little shaky, she stood. "Luke, I'm okay. I promise, you didn't hurt me." She was relieved that her voice seemed much steadier than she actually felt. Although she wanted to go to him, she sensed his withdrawal and knew he would recoil from her touch. Instead she placed a hand on the door frame to make certain her wobbly legs would keep her upright.

He stared at her for a moment longer, as if trying to ensure she was being truthful. Finally satisfied in that regard, he turned his back to her, walked to the far window and opened it, allowing the cool air in. He leaned his head against the window and said quietly, "Please go."

"Luke, you were having a nightmare. Can we talk—"

"No. It's over. Please go."

"But, if you talk to—" she pleaded.

"Claire, I need you to leave, now. Please go to bed." His voice was weary and the words were emotionless. He continued to stare out of the window. "We can talk in the morning."

Sensing his pain but feeling shut out, Claire felt tears form in her eyes. Reluctantly she slipped out of his room, closing the door and leaving him alone.

THE NEXT MORNING was gray and significantly cooler, closely mirroring Claire's emotions. After returning to her room, she'd had a great deal of difficulty going back to sleep. When she'd first been awakened by Luke's cries, she'd assumed it was nearly dawn. But she'd been surprised to see that it was only two o'clock. She spent the next hours tossing in her bed, alternately listening for more indications of Luke's night terrors and trying to think through what to do to help him.

Her emotions had run the gamut from deep despair that their relationship was over, to quiet confidence that in the morning they would calmly and sensibly discuss what had occurred. In that scenario, she would convince Luke to share the nightmare and together they could identify the possible causes. Her mind raced, trying to remember all that she had studied about veterans' health problems. She wondered about what he might have seen or heard or done—what he'd been exposed to during his multiple deployments in the Persian Gulf. She recalled that he'd actually been in Afghanistan for a while and wondered if he was experiencing PTSD.

As the night progressed, she became more and more certain that she could help. After all, she was an expert in taking care of the mental and emotional problems that often accompanied children with severe health issues. Translating that knowledge to caring for a healthy young man couldn't be that difficult, could it? She knew that it was vital to draw him out the next morning. He needed to talk to her, to trust her.

She could help him. She *would* help him. She knew that he cared for her—he loved her.

So he would listen.

At about four, she'd finally dozed off,

sleeping fitfully. She awoke a few hours later to the gray gloom from the bedroom window. She showered and dressed casually in worn jeans and a light blue blouse, grateful that the bruises she'd expected were hidden. She pulled her hair back in a pony tail and put on her glasses. Glancing in the mirror, she decided that she looked better than she felt. Fortunately, the poor night's sleep wasn't obvious.

She knew Luke was still in the apartment as she could hear him through the closed door. She sensed that the next minutes were among the most important in their relationship. Finally, eager to see him and talk to him, she took a deep breath, said a short prayer and left the bedroom.

LUKE WAS SITTING at the table, as she'd expected he would be. All four of the computers were active. He only glanced at her as she entered the room. He didn't speak, but returned his attention to one of the monitors.

Claire studied him for a moment and was discouraged by what she saw. He looked terrible. He was still wearing the ratty gym shorts from last night, but he'd thrown on an equally ratty, faded T-shirt. He hadn't shaved and his hair was lank and uncombed. His eyes were red-rimmed, with dark spots under each. She suspected he hadn't slept at all.

"Good morning." Claire tried to sound cheerful, but the greeting came out flat.

"Morning," he replied gruffly. He didn't look up.

Trying to regain normalcy, Claire moved toward the kitchen. "Have you had breakfast?"

"No, I'm not really hungry." He waited a span and evidently thought he needed to add something. "You go ahead."

"How about coffee?" She looked at the nearly empty coffee pot; its contents closely resembled sludge. "I can make some fresh."

Luke frowned at his drained cup and then glanced at Claire. "Yeah, okay." His focus moved to another of the computers and he tapped at its keyboard. His manner was dismissive; it was blatantly obvious that he didn't want to talk.

The silence grew awkward as Claire

puttered in the kitchen making coffee and Luke appeared to study his computers. When the coffee was ready, Claire poured two cups and carried them to the dining area, placing one in front of Luke before sitting down across from him. She watched him for a couple of minutes. His brow was slightly creased and he seemed to be working very hard to maintain his concentration and ignore her.

Needing to start a conversation, she finally asked, "Is everything all right with the moving missile?"

"Yeah, we identified it and were able to pinpoint its source. We're pretty sure where it's going." He continued to type. "At any rate, it's in the government officials' and diplomats' hands now. We'll probably be hearing about new disarmament 'talks' in the news over the next few days."

"Oh." She took a sip of coffee. "So nothing to worry about, then?" She wasn't particularly concerned; she just wanted him to talk to her.

"No. Pretty much the same old stuff." A soft ping from one of the computers caught Luke's attention. He shifted to a different screen, moved the mouse and clicked on an icon. "Good," he said absently, then returned his attention to the monitor he'd been checking previously. He clicked a few more keys and then glanced across to Claire. "Just got a response from Bridgette—you know, Brad's fiancée. I sent her a note earlier asking if you could stay with her for a while." He gestured to the computer. "She just sent me an email saying that would be fine. She said she'd love to have you." He looked away again.

Claire was stunned. The feeling in her stomach was similar to what she'd felt the previous night when she'd been slammed against the door jamb. Actually this pain was much worse. Almost a minute passed before she could respond. "You want me to leave?"

Finally, Luke stopped typing. His eyes rose to hers and his hands moved to rest in his lap. "Yes, Claire, I do." His face was expressionless. He licked his lips and seemed to want to say something else, but decided against it.

"But, why?" She blinked hard several

times, determined to avoid tears. "Luke, if it's about last night—I swear, you didn't hurt me." She moved close to where he still sat and tried to add a little humor into the discussion. "When I was skating, I fell ten to twenty times each session. Talk about bruises, sprains, cuts and whatever. I promise that was much harder…" The corners of her lips rose a little as she tried to smile, but the smile fell flat when he only continued to stare.

After a moment, he shook his head in denial, but his expression warred with his words. "Look, I have a lot to do in a short while—getting ready to leave and all. It would be best for me to not have to worry about you." His eyes were tormented and couldn't hold hers. Finally, he looked at his coffee and added, "You should stay with Bridgette until you're allowed to go back home."

"Luke, if it's the nightmare, maybe if you would tell me about it—"

"No! I'm not going to talk about last night…except to apologize again." His tone softened slightly as he continued. "I truly regret… I think you know I would never intentionally…" His jaw clenched and abruptly he pushed away from the table and stood. He picked up his coffee and started to his room. Without looking back he said, "You can pack while I shower and dress. I'll drop you by Bridgette's on my way to work." He closed the bedroom door without waiting for a response.

Claire no longer tried to stop the tears. They flowed freely as she rose and returned to Brad's room and hurriedly packed her belongings.

She was dry-eyed, however, when Luke emerged from his room a half hour later. He had showered and dressed in his "office" uniform. Despite the haggard lines around his eyes, undoubtedly due to his lack of sleep, he looked beautiful to her, and she had to bite her lip hard to keep the tears that were threatening again in check.

Luke looked miserable when he carried Claire's bag to the door of Bridgette's apartment. When Bridgette answered his knock, he gave her a quick hug, a muttered "thanks" and a promise to be in touch before retreating to his borrowed vehicle.

He didn't even look at Claire.

CHAPTER THIRTEEN

CLAIRE AND BRIDGETTE shared many similar values, experiences and interests. Since both were nurses and both were in love with military officers, they had a great deal to talk about. Whereas Claire was quiet and reserved, Bridgette was outgoing, and she quickly made Claire feel at ease and ready to talk.

Over coffee the first morning, Claire learned that Bridgette's father was a career Army officer and her family had followed him all over the world. His last assignment had been in Korea and Bridgette had migrated to Seoul after completing her nursing education in the U.S.

Bridgette took a sip of her latte. "About a year after I got here, Dad decided to retire, and he and Mom moved home to Kansas City. Of course, they assumed I would go with them, but there was a development—Bradley Littlejohn." She beamed when she mentioned his name. "Brad is an Air Force captain and he's absolutely crazy about me."

Bridgette sighed and peered at her new friend over her coffee cup. Claire could see that because of her happiness, Bridgette wanted the same for all her friends.

"Okay, I've talked enough. Your turn. Luke didn't tell me why he wanted you to stay here. Yesterday, you both seemed like...well, like things couldn't be going better. Did you guys have a fight or something?"

"No, not really." Claire stared into her coffee cup. "Luke told me he needed me to stay here because he has a lot to do. He was going to be busy and..." Claire wondered if she looked as despondent as she sounded.

Bridgette persisted. "Do you think he was getting cold feet? Maybe because your relationship was moving too fast?"

"No, that's not the problem. I think he was fine with our relationship. He was very happy—that was pretty obvious—until..." She sighed and told Bridgette about Luke's nightmare and what had transpired the night before.

"It's not about having a relationship at all…" She stared at her hands. Her words were quiet. "I think he's afraid of himself. He thought he'd hurt me. He hadn't, of course—well just a couple of bruises… but it scared him—a lot. That, plus whatever is giving him the nightmares. He was in pretty bad shape, but he wouldn't talk about it…" She stopped. "I feel awkward discussing it with you, like I'm sharing something personal, but I want to help him. Besides I'm mad at him for pushing me away. I believe—no, I *know* he loves me, but he's afraid…"

Bridgette was sympathetic. "Don't worry. I know how he talked about you before he even asked you out—he was hooked on you from the beginning. And I saw the way he looked at you when he dropped you off—I've never seen a more unhappy man." She actually smiled then. "He'll come around." She patted Claire's hand and said, "He's not stupid. He knows that you care about him. Besides, he can't go through the rest of his life alone because he's worried about what he *might* do in his sleep."

BRIDGETTE WORKED EVENINGS at the base hospital's emergency department, and during the next few days she spent the daytime hours with Claire, shopping at the base stores, going to yoga class, jogging and having coffee or lunch with other friends. The evenings tended to be very lonely and while Bridgette was at the hospital, Claire spent time working on her data analysis, reading and occasionally trying to watch television. She checked on Jessica's recovery, followed up on the children at Samsung, and called her parents daily.

Often, though, her mind turned to Luke. She tried to imagine what he was doing and wondered if he was as unhappy as she. In contrast, she rarely thought about the reason for her confinement on the base. She felt safe, although very restricted, in the highly secure environment, and chose to ignore the fact that there had been two serious threats to her life.

On the fourth morning she spent at Bridgette's, the pair was again sipping coffee on the small patio behind the apartment. The weather was still a little cool but the sky was clear. Inevitably, the topic of Claire's relationship with Luke came up.

"So, did he call last night?" Bridgette asked as she turned her face toward the morning sun.

Not needing to ask who "he" was, Claire shook her head in disappointment and said, "No. He hasn't called. I haven't talked to him since he dropped me here on Monday. He's sent a couple of emails—really brief and to the point—telling me when my passport would be in and saying he's still waiting to hear from one of his colleagues about my adoption." She sipped her coffee.

"One kind of fun thing is that Tony Mancini—the marine who works with Luke at the embassy—has stopped by several times to see Jessica. They're actually coming here tomorrow to take me to lunch." She was smiling. "After I got the email, I called Jessica and she told me that Tony is really cute and sweet and funny and he seems to be crazy about her. I think it's one of those 'opposites attract' things..."

"So, speaking of guys being crazy...

What gives with Luke not calling or coming by? I would have thought he'd cave by now."

"Me too… Or at least I had hoped so. I've thought about trying to come up with something, a reason to call him, but…"

Bridgette shook her head and sighed, "Men…"

They didn't speak for a few minutes. Suddenly, Bridgette put down her mug and slapped the table with her hand. "I know what you need—let's go shopping!" Her green eyes sparkled. "Let me think… Purses or shoes? I know of about five different shops on Itaewon where we can get some great shoes at terrific prices!"

Claire brightened considerably. "I haven't been to work in nearly a week and I'd love to get out and go somewhere off base." She looked at her watch. It was just after ten. The idea of a shopping trip to Itaewon with Bridgette was hugely appealing. She drummed her fingers on the patio table and thought out loud. "I think it'll be safe to leave Yongsan for a couple of hours, don't you? The attacks were both at night and besides, they knew where I would be."

Bridgette nodded. "If they are still interested in finding you, they don't know where you are," she rationalized. "And even if they know you're at Yongsan, they wouldn't know if you left for a while."

Claire picked up her train of thought. "We could leave by walking out one of the gates and they couldn't possibly know where we were off to."

Bridgette ended the discussion. "No, there's no way they would know." She stood and reached for her purse. "There's this great little tea house where we can go for lunch after the shoes… I promise I'll have you home by three—since I have to go to work!"

"Let's do it!" Claire copied Bridgette's action, picking up her purse and heading to the door. "When Luke and I were walking the other evening, I saw this really cute bag in one of the windows that my mom would love. And her birthday is coming up…"

THE SHOPPING TRIP was a much-needed respite from Claire's recent solitude. Bridgette proved to be an excellent companion and astute shopper, and by one o'clock, they had each bought a new purse. Claire also found a lovely silk scarf for her mother and Bridgette bought a pair of black suede half boots. At the Japanese tea house they stuffed their shopping bags under the table and talked about nursing, the men in their lives and Bridgette's wedding plans.

Between sips of almond tea and bites of salmon, Bridgette told Claire how she and Brad met. "He came into the emergency room after spraining his ankle sliding into home during a base-league softball game. We started talking and he asked me out right then." She grinned. "He was cute and funny and crazy about me! That was in November. He proposed Christmas." She studied her ring proudly.

"Do you have a date?" Claire asked, as she munched on her shrimp salad.

"June 30. Brad was just promoted to major and he's been reassigned. In about a month we'll head back to Missouri for the wedding and then we'll be moving to Germany." Her new friend's happiness gave Claire a twinge of envy. That was quickly replaced by new resolve. She wouldn't let Luke push her away without a fight!

After lunch, it was time to head back to the base. As the women left the tea house they were laughing over an anecdote Bridgette had shared about a recent E.D. visit from two brothers who had dared each other to put pebbles in their noses. Even though the distance back to Yongsan was relatively short, they decided to take a taxi so they wouldn't have to walk while trying to carry their shopping bags.

Standing by the curb, Claire raised her hand for a cab. Several sped by, each with passengers in the rear. They continued to wait as a late-model black sedan slowed down and pulled toward the curb. Assuming the vehicle was stopping to let someone out, the women stepped back a couple of paces and continued their conversation.

Both doors on the passenger side opened wide and two men emerged, lunging at Claire. The man who'd been in the back seat grabbed Claire's left arm, causing her to drop her shopping bags. Almost simultaneously, the second man caught her other arm and began pushing her toward the open rear door. Without conscious thought, Claire buckled her knees and dropped to the ground, landing hard on her bottom. Sitting on the sidewalk, she straightened her legs and pushed back against the men who were trying to force her forward.

"No! Stop it!" she yelled, as she struggled to throw off their hands.

Bridgette screeched, "Stop! Get away!" She gathered the neck of the shopping bag that held her boots and swung it as hard as she could at the head of the man closer to her.

Claire heard a muffled "thunk" and suddenly the man on her right stumbled back toward the car. The unexpected blow caused him to trip as one foot teetered off the curb. Unable to stop his forward motion, he rammed into the rear car door, slamming it shut. The man pulling on Claire's left arm let out a hoarse scream and abruptly let go of her. He'd been holding on to the car's door frame, trying to gain leverage to drag Claire toward the vehicle. His hand was now caught and the other man—the one from the front seat— was trying to regain his balance. The slamming door and resultant scream evidently fractured the driver's attention. The car lurched forward a couple of feet, dragging the guy whose hand was caught into the other man, causing him to trip and fall. The incident might have been comical, had the two women not been terrified by the attempted kidnapping.

Several people were staring at the altercation, and an older man stopped to help Claire to her feet. She thanked him, grabbed her bags and backed away from the curb.

With her free hand, Claire grabbed Bridgette's arm and pulled her toward the shops, into the growing crowd. "Let's get out of here!" she panted. Her heart was racing and a now familiar fear settled on her as they ran quickly up the street, in the opposite direction of the way the car had been headed.

Neither woman looked back and within a minute they had cleared the end of the block and turned the corner. Quickly, they covered another two blocks, winding through the narrow side streets before finally stopping in an alleyway behind some two- and three-story dwellings. Only a few people were in sight and no one seemed to be paying attention to them.

Breathing heavily, Claire managed to say, "Are you okay?"

"Yeah, fine... Scared the snot out of me though!" Bridgette gasped. "We need to call somebody... The police? Or maybe the embassy?"

Claire had already pulled out her cell phone. "I've got it." Not sure whom else to call, she dialed Luke's number.

LUKE WAS IN a bad mood, which was unusual. About lunchtime, he told the duty sergeant he had some personal business to attend to and gave instructions to call should something come up. Noting Luke's scowl, the sergeant had readily agreed.

Luke first went to his apartment and tried to work. He found himself at the door of Brad's room, staring at nothing in particular. The room was once again meticulously neat and bore no visible signs of its recent occupant. But he could still smell Claire's lotion, and his mood degraded even further.

Finally, he gave up his private struggle and went to Bridgette's apartment, telling himself he would just check on Claire to see how she was doing. But when he got there, no one answered his knock. That led to a search of the base. He went by stores and restaurants, but the women were not to be found. Several times he thought about giving up and calling her, but he'd told himself that would be surrendering his previous resolve. Finally he returned to Bridgette's apartment and sat on the front step of the building, waiting with escalating impatience.

When his phone rang, Luke immediately recognized Claire's number and answered the call before the end of the first ring.

"Where are you?" His tone was brusque. "I went to—"

"Thank God!" she said, wanting to weep with relief. "Luke, it happened again! Some men tried to push me into a car, but Bridgette hit one and then the other got his hand stuck, and then the car pulled up and dragged the first man into the second man and we ran away..." She didn't realize she was babbling.

Luke stood. *"Where—are—you?"*

"We were on Itaewon. We went shopping and had tea." She was still anxious but her panic seemed to be easing. "Luke, they found me! How?"

He waited just a breath, considering her question. A notion occurred to him and he muttered, "Shoot! They must have accessed the GPS chip or managed to triangulate the location of the number." There was a brief pause then his words became very distinct. "Claire, it's your phone. You have to lose your phone…" Another second passed, then he said, "Claire, listen carefully. Where are you now?" His words were unemotional; he wanted to keep her calm.

"Behind some buildings, several blocks off Itaewon."

"Okay, I'm going to come get you. Can you meet me at our restaurant—you know which one?" He started jogging toward his vehicle.

"Yes, I remember where—"

"Good, I'll come pick you up there. But first, you and Bridgette need to change your appearance. Simple changes are fine.

Just take off a sweater or put on a different color shirt."

"Okay—"

"And cover Bridgette's hair…"

Claire glanced at her friend's dark red hair and answered, "Yes, I see."

"Claire, you've got to lose the phone *now*—so they won't be able to find you again. Try to put it on or in something moving, okay? Do you understand?"

"Yes—"

"I'm on my way," he spat before hanging up.

CLAIRE TURNED TO BRIDGETTE, who was standing very close. "Did you hear?"

Bridgette nodded. Heeding Luke's instructions, she had already taken off her cream-colored sweater and stuffed it into one of her shopping bags. Claire dug through one of her own bags, pulled out the silk scarf and handed it to her friend. Bridgette threw it over her head, tying it under her chin.

"Let's go," Claire prompted. "When we pass a shop, I'll pick up something to cover my shirt."

They hurried to the end of the alley. Traffic on the narrow cross street was moving slowly and Claire ventured into the street, creeping behind a small delivery truck that was loaded with wooden crates. Without pausing, she dropped her cell into the bed of the vehicle, which edged forward to the stoplight.

Bridgette had followed her, and the two women crossed the side street and continued to make their way back to bustling Itaewon, all the while being wary of black sedans. As they got closer, they ducked into a small ladies' clothing store and Claire quickly pulled a black cotton blouse off a rack and took it to the counter. She paid cash and slipped the garment over her yellow silk top as they walked out the door.

Back on Itaewon, the women's confidence grew a little. Claire pointed down the street. "That's the Starbucks we went to the other night. I think the Italian restaurant is this way." Calmer now, they made their way up the busy street, staying as far from the cars as possible, practically hugging the buildings and trying to hide among the crowds of people.

FIFTEEN MINUTES AFTER Luke answered the terrifying phone call, he pulled up in front of the Italian restaurant in a borrowed Toyota. It was a minor miracle that he'd managed the short trip—swerving wildly through heavy city traffic—without getting into an accident. Not caring about collecting a fine, he parked illegally, and left the vehicle.

During the short drive, he'd been only marginally successful in managing his panicky thoughts. His mind had raced through all sorts of scenarios. What if he was too late? Claire could be injured... She could be bleeding on a back street... She could be locked in a car with strange men taking her someplace where he'd never find her...

She could be dead...

His heart pounded painfully as he tried to curtail the vivid images. *She's all right*, he told himself over and over. *Please,* he prayed repeatedly, *please let her be okay!*

He was furious with Claire for leaving

the base and putting herself at risk. Alternating with the terrified thoughts, he considered all the things he would say and do when he found her safe. He would rant, scold, chastise. He wanted to yell at her for putting him through this awful fear. He wanted to crush her to him, hold her and never let her out of his sight again.

He scoured the street in front of the restaurant, but the women were nowhere to be seen. In short order he rushed through the door, hoping they'd be inside. Trying to tamp down his terror, he hurriedly searched the patrons, but Claire and Bridgette weren't there.

Oh, no, he thought, *they should already be here!* Cold sweat drenched his body. Reluctantly, he retreated onto the busy sidewalk and scanned all directions again. He had decided to re-enter the restaurant when he caught sight of Claire and Bridgette. They had turned a corner from a side street onto Itaewon—directly across the street from where he stood. Claire spotted him simultaneously and waved. Seeing her left him weak-kneed and dizzy.

Clutching each other and looking harried, the women waited for the light to change before hurrying across to meet a very relieved and very angry Luke. The moment Claire set foot on the curb, Luke crushed her to his chest, reveling in the joy of actually touching her. He closed his eyes, buried his face in her hair, and gave a quick prayer of thanksgiving.

His heart was still beating erratically and his palms were sweating, but he managed to rein back his fury for a moment to assess both women. Pulling away, he noticed that Claire was wearing a too large dark shirt over her jeans and yellow blouse, both of which appeared to be stained with dirt and grime. Her black hair was mussed, and she pushed it back with a trembling hand. He didn't detect any obvious injuries and reluctantly let her go, turning to Bridgette. Other than her rapid breathing and still frightened look, she also seemed to be all right. Her hair was covered by a printed scarf of gray-and-pink silk which clashed dreadfully with her light green blouse.

"Are ya'll okay?" he finally asked.

Both women nodded, but Bridgette looked very pale.

"Let's get out of here." Luke motioned to the Toyota compact parked nearby. He ushered Bridgette into the back seat, then placed Claire beside him in the passenger's side. Within a minute he'd folded himself into the driver's seat and pulled the vehicle into traffic.

Now that Luke's fear had been alleviated, his anger returned. He glared at Claire and said, "What were you thinking leaving Yongsan? You *knew* better." His jaw tightened and his voice intensified. "I *told* you to *stay* on base. You knew better than to go somewhere without a bodyguard!"

The rapid transition from abject terror to profound relief had left Claire stunned. Faced now with Luke's wrath, she was unable to contain her emotions. "I…I'm so sorry, Luke… We…er…I thought it would be okay." Tears slid down her cheeks. "I was, er…I wasn't…" Her voice trailed off and she barely managed to stifle a sob.

A subdued Bridgette spoke up from the backseat. "We wanted to get out. I thought a shopping trip would be fun… Luke, we didn't have any idea there would be a way the…er…bad guys *could* find Claire."

Luke glanced at Claire's stricken face and his temper abated. He reached over to gently rub away a tear and he sighed audibly. "Look, we'll discuss that later. Right now, I need you to tell me exactly what happened."

The women took several minutes to recount the events of the afternoon. They explained how everything had seemed perfectly fine until the two men jumped out of a black car and tried to abduct Claire.

Luke was watching the traffic, but he could feel Claire watching him throughout their recitation of the events. When they detailed how she'd dropped to the ground as the two men pulled on her arms, he couldn't help tensing his jaw. When Bridgette described how she'd used her boots as a club, he could feel one corner of his mouth turning up slightly. Then he actually snickered upon learning that the last thing Claire and Bridgette saw as they ran were the two men being dragged in the gutter as the driver rolled forward.

After they'd finished describing the incident, he just shook his head and sighed. Glancing at the redheaded nurse in the rearview mirror, he said, "Bridgette, that was fast thinking. Thank you for having the guts to use your boots as a weapon instead of running away." His attention moved to Claire and he muttered, "And thank God you're so stubborn. If…" His eyes returned to the street and he refused to finish the comment.

Bridgette suddenly noticed their surroundings. "Where are we going? This isn't the way to the base."

"We're headed to the police station by Seoul National University. I called Detective Kang on my way to pick you up… We've got an appointment."

Captain Choi and Detective Kang were waiting when the trio arrived. As they had the previous week, Luke, Claire and now Bridgette took seats in the detective's office. The women related the story they had just told Luke and the two policemen peppered them with questions.

Luke was quiet and somehow managed

to maintain his composure throughout. As they were concluding the interview, Captain Choi said, "We will put out an alert to all of the area emergency departments to watch for men with the injuries you describe. We may get lucky. I will also have officers search the area stores to see if there are any security cameras pointed in the direction of the altercation. Most likely there will not be, as the cameras are usually focused near their shop's doors and don't scan all the way to the street. I will let you know if we find anything."

"There is another development you might want to look into," Luke told the officers. "We may have learned why Claire is being targeted."

With Luke's encouragement, Claire explained how she had contacted the adoption agency after her arrival in Seoul. She provided them with her birth date and the name of the agency in Seattle. Her voice was quiet, and she was subdued when she finished.

Both Detective Kang and Captain Choi seemed to be relieved that a potential motive had been identified. "Detective Kang will contact the agency today to see what he can learn about your adoption, Ms. Olsen."

As they rose to leave, Luke addressed Choi. "One more thing, Captain. This is the third attack. They are obviously determined and capable enough to obtain her personal information and use sophisticated electronic tracking. Ms. Olsen needs to go where she will be safe. When will you pull the hold on her passport and allow her to leave the country?"

The captain returned Luke's stare and answered politely. "Lieutenant, I understand your concern. This attack and the new information makes us even more resolved to find out who wishes her harm. But if we are not successful, I will remove the hold one week at the latest." He shook his head and frowned at Claire. Still speaking to Luke, however, he said, "It was my understanding that she would remain with you at Yongsan. She should not have left where she was safe without an escort."

"Yes, I know." Luke's lips thinned and he practically glared at Claire as he answered, "It won't happen again."

CHAPTER FOURTEEN

THE TRIO WAS subdued during the drive back to the base. Luke parked in front of Bridgette's apartment building and both women started to exit, but he reached across the front seat to clasp Claire's arm. "No," he said. "Stay put for now. I'll bring you back later." His voice was flat.

Claire's heart rate had pretty much returned to normal, but the look in Luke's eyes set her nerves on edge once again. His solemn expression led her to consider that his anger had only been restrained for Bridgette's sake and that when they were alone she would be strongly chastised for her actions.

Luke handed Bridgette her bags and hugged her. His voice broke a little as he said, "Thank you again. If you hadn't intervened, I don't know... Brad's a lucky guy."

Bridgette gave him a small smile as she blinked back tears. She kissed him on the cheek before turning and going inside.

Luke was silent during the short drive across the base. He opened Claire's door and held on to her arm as he ushered her into his apartment. Although his touch was gentle, his grasp was firm as he led her to one of the chairs at the cluttered kitchen table and impatiently motioned for her to sit. His jaw clenched and his mouth thinned as he stared at her a moment. He scrubbed a hand over his face and grumbled, "I can't think when I'm looking at you." He turned away and paced across the room.

Claire didn't blame Luke for being angry. What she and Bridgette had done was stupid. They had ignored his orders, and as a result, both had been endangered and she could have easily been kidnapped and very possibly killed by now. She hadn't completely recovered from the fright and remained quiet.

Staring out the window onto the parking lot, Luke said, "I don't know what to do with you…" Fury and impatience were apparent, even though the words were quietly spoken.

"Luke, I'm so sorry—"

"What if they'd been successful? What if they had pulled you into that car?" He leaned his head against the window and closed his eyes. "Do you know what they might have done to you?" The last was said in a whisper.

"Luke, I'm sorry. I was stupid. But I didn't think they could... I'm sorry..." She blinked several times, trying to keep from crying.

He simply stared out the window for a bit longer and sighed again. "This isn't working, either." He turned around and glared at her, repeating with exasperation, "What am I going to do with you?"

"Luke, I'll stay at Bridgette's. I promise I won't leave the base again without some type of escort."

His frown deepened and he blinked. The anger had evaporated. "That's not what I'm talking about." He shook his head and confessed, "I can't handle this. I tried to stay away from you, but it seems I can't..."

"Luke, you don't have to. There's no reason…" She rose and took a step toward him, but he put up his hands, halting her.

"No. Stay there!" His voice was agitated. They stood several feet apart for a moment. Finally Luke rubbed the back of his neck with frustration. "Claire, look at me!" He held his hands out at his side, bringing her attention to the wide span between his arms and the imposing breadth of his chest. "Really look at me! I hit you… I could have hurt you!" He was practically shouting now. "Claire, *I* might have killed you!"

"Luke, you were asleep!" she cried. "You weren't trying to hurt me! It was a nightmare!"

He dropped his hands and looked at her pleadingly. "Don't you see that I can't be around you and not want to be with you? I want to marry you!" He shook his head in defeat. "But I can't trust myself… What if…"

In a breath, Claire's frown morphed into a blinding smile. She took a step toward him.

He stepped back. He looked as panicked as if he'd suddenly discovered she was radioactive. "No, you stay there." He held up his hand to hold her away.

"Luke, it's okay." Her eyes sparkled. "You won't hurt me."

"You can't know that." He backed up farther.

"I trust you." She continued to advance. "I think you weren't expecting me that night—unconsciously, I mean. If you were expecting me—if you were used to me, I think you wouldn't have reacted as you did."

"You can't know that!" he repeated with anger. "I have to sleep sometime, and I don't think I could if you were anywhere near." The wall halted his retreat.

Claire followed. "Luke, I love you. Not being here with you was much more painful than any fall. Please, let me stay. We can work it out."

She stopped her pursuit only inches from him. He was so big that all she could see was the top buttons of his uniform shirt. He was standing rigid with his hands at his side, still determined to keep his distance. But she leaned into him, and her hands skimmed their way up his hard chest to gently touch his face. Her eyes followed the path of her hands, rising to catch and hold his. Her hands came to rest behind his neck and she pulled lightly, hoping and praying he would acquiesce.

LUKE HAD BEEN RUNNING hard and fast, trying to get away from her. He told himself it was for her protection, and it was. But he was smart enough to recognize that he couldn't keep retreating from her—or from what he was feeling. He didn't want to.

Luke wanted this woman more than he'd ever wanted anything in his life, and he couldn't keep running. Pushing her away had only endangered her once again.

He stared at her beautiful eyes and sighed raggedly. His arms left his sides and encircled her, clutching her tightly, desperately. Resignation and wonder combined in a sigh as he leaned down to kiss her. The kiss was soft and loving, gentle and searching. It wanted and demanded nothing but to be shared.

With a cry that was part anger, part elation and complete capitulation, he lifted her off the ground and surrendered. He touched her face and her hair. He ran his hands up her arms in a loving caress. "You win," he whispered. "I can't fight us both." He framed her face with both hands and took her mouth with his.

AT FIRST, CLAIRE WAS STUNNED. She felt the change in him and it was frightening. Her legs were no longer supporting her, and she was forced to cling to him. She was literally overwhelmed by his size and power. The hardness and bulk of his arms and shoulders and chest were alarming, and she had to remind herself that he wouldn't harm her. His hands might be big and strong, but they were gentle and loving. His size was intimidating, but he knew the limits of his strength. With that realization she gave in and allowed herself to be carried away.

Finally Luke's kisses gentled. His mouth moved from hers to touch her temple and then her hair. His arms relaxed and his hands loosened from their almost desperate grasp to lightly clasp her upper arms. He kissed her forehead as he pushed her away.

"We need to talk," Luke said, taking her hand and leading her to the sofa. He pulled her into his arms and they sat together, reveling in being close, being in love.

Clasping his hand, Claire searched his eyes. "Tell me about the nightmares."

He froze and immediately pulled back. "No, I don't want to talk about that."

"Why? Luke, you can tell me anything."

He moved restlessly then pulled his eyes away from hers to stare toward the far side of the room. "There's really nothing to tell."

"Have you had them before?"

He ran his hands through his hair. "You're not going to drop it, are you?"

"No. You need to talk about it. If not to me, to someone… You haven't, have you?"

"Talked to anyone? No." He glanced at her, but quickly his eyes shifted toward the blackened television. "Claire, it's nothing, really…"

"But you were worried enough to push me away."

He sighed. "It starts off the same every

time. I'm back outside of Kandahar… I'm on patrol with the team—which is kind of odd, because I very rarely went on patrol when I was stationed there. In reality I was the 'computer geek.' For the most part I just stayed put, sorting out the data we collected from satellites, drones and informants… I actually do a lot more patrolling here."

He looked at her and then at the coffee table. "Anyway, in the nightmares, I'm on patrol and we've come to a road that splits. Suddenly we become aware that we're being ambushed. We don't know which way to go—we can't go back and we can't go forward. We know there are IEDs or mines everywhere."

He shifted and glanced at her. "This is where it changes—sometimes I'm the officer in charge and am responsible—I'm supposed to give orders, but I don't know what to do. I know that men will live or die based on what I say. Other times, I'm following orders… I'm on the radio calling for backup, but I know I'm too late. We need to move, but I can't get a response, and I don't know what to tell the guys to do…"

He gave a short, rueful laugh and shook his head. "Claire, the funny thing is that none of this ever happened. And it's even funnier—actually not funny, but aggravating—because I know it's a dream. I know it's not happening, but it's so real that I panic. In the dream, it's my responsibility to keep everyone safe…"

She took his hand and rubbed his fingers lightly with hers. "So you were never in an ambush? You were never attacked?"

"No." The answer was short, then he added, "Actually, all of the patrols I was on were very non-eventful."

"Are you sure?"

He looked angry again. "Yes, doctor, I'm sure. Nothing like that ever happened. We were always very much on guard and scared spitless, but I promise we were never attacked."

"Luke, I'm sorry, I didn't mean…"

"Honey, I know what you're thinking. It's understandable… You think I was in some sort of confrontation or battle and am suffering from PTSD." He stood then and paced away. "You may be thinking that I have 'repressed memories'—that my mind has suppressed something terrible." He turned to face her and shrugged. "That's not the case. In the nine months I was in Afghanistan—on the front lines, so to speak—I never once fired my weapon except in training situations, and I never really came under fire. There were a couple of instances when snipers fired random shots at us, but nothing even came close."

He stopped and threw up his hands in surrender or frustration, Claire couldn't tell which. "I was never directly in danger. I never saw any of my colleagues shot or hit by an IED or anything even remotely like that. My only exposure was some of the stories I heard or read about." He shook his head and fell silent again.

"So why do you think you dream about something that never happened?" Her voice was quiet.

He sighed and looked a little calmer. "Who knows? Even though I was never personally involved with an—um…a situation—we had to be constantly vigilant—

and I mean *constantly*. It takes a lot out of you mentally, physically and emotionally."

Claire tried to convey her love and empathy with her eyes. But Luke was angered anew by something he saw in her expression. "Claire, I don't want pity. I don't want you to feel sorry for me. There's nothing to feel sorry for! I'm not helpless or a child. I'm not hurt…" He sighed and pinched the bridge of his nose in frustration. "Some of those guys—in real life…"

Claire chose to ignore his tirade. "Luke, do you feel guilty about anything?"

He actually scoffed then and answered quickly. "No. You have to believe me on this one, too. My work is all about surveillance and intelligence. Anything I might feel guilty about would be something I missed or something I miscalled. I don't know of anything that fits either category, but then, I don't know what I don't know…" He looked pensive and even somewhat remorseful. "Of course, I understand that some of my analyses and reports likely contributed to military actions—that's part of the deal. People have probably been hurt or even killed as a result. We're always aware of that and learn to live with it…"

They were silent for a while. Claire continued to hold his hand, silently giving him comfort. Finally she said, "How often do you have the nightmares?"

He gave a short laugh. "Actually, I don't have a clue. I only know that every two or three weeks I'll wake up terrified, sweating and with my heart racing. Once, I actually woke up in the living room.

"A little more often, I'll wake up and know I've had a bad night, but I don't directly remember the dream… And then on a couple of occasions, Brad has mentioned that he heard me yelling or groaning in my sleep."

"Brad actually heard you yelling and didn't do anything except tell you the next morning?" Claire couldn't help sounding incredulous.

Luke gave her an aggravated look then answered with ire. "Honey, Brad's not stupid enough to approach me in the dark when I'm not awake and aware." He looked at her accusingly, still raw from talking about his weaknesses. "And now that you remind me, I found Brad's bat on the floor. What do you think you were going to do with that?"

Claire was hurt and more than a little insulted by his comment. But she straightened her spine and answered, "I thought you were being attacked. I wanted to help you, and that was the only weapon I could find."

"So you were going to use a *baseball bat* to defend me against some unknown number of attackers? Do you have a *clue* how dumb that was? Honey, it would take at *least* two, but probably three or four men to hold me down. And you burst in with a baseball bat?"

Claire blinked several times, trying to hold back the tears caused by his biting words. Managing to keep her voice calm, she answered, "You're right of course. It was stupid on several levels." She bit her lip then added, "I guess I've sometimes rushed into action without thinking... I thought you were being hurt. I couldn't stay away."

Luke shoved his hands in his pockets and remained silent.

"And you know the *really* stupid thing?" Claire's hurt morphed into exasperation. Tears slipped down her cheeks, but despite that suggestion of weakness, she turned to him and poked him on the chest with her finger. "I'd do it again. If I ever, under any circumstance, thought you were in danger, I'd do *anything* I could to protect you."

LUKE WAS SUDDENLY REMINDED of the video of Claire fighting back against two armed men. That memory and her quiet declaration caused him to clench his jaw and swallow hard. His own anger deflated like a burst balloon. He took a calming breath and then another. Finally he looked at her and sighed. She stiffened when he pulled her into his arms and buried his face in her hair.

"What am I going to do with you?" His words were quiet. "Claire, I'm sorry. Truly sorry—that was unfair and uncalled for. You weren't stupid. You were brave—very brave. Well, okay, on reflection maybe you were brave *and* stupid." He pulled back and smiled pleadingly down at her. "I'm sorry I was a jerk. You hit a nerve by making me talk about the nightmares, and honestly, I'm not even sure what the nerve was." He smoothed her hair and touched her lips with his. "Will you forgive me?"

She blinked at him and rolled her lips until they became a reluctant smile. "Yes, but only because you're cute when you apologize." She raised her arms to encircle his neck and kissed the corner of his mouth. "One more thing before we completely drop it, though." She looked serious again. "Would you consider talking to someone—a counselor I mean?" She sounded hopeful.

Luke sobered and he sighed. "Okay, I'll think about it, but I don't believe it's necessary. I swear, I don't know what's causing the nightmares. I've never been directly exposed to anything that normally results in PTSD. The nightmares are likely just the result of the need to be hyper vigilant at all times when I was in Kandahar." He kissed her forehead again. "I think—well, I hope—they'll just go away. But, I'll consider talking to a counselor."

She searched his face. "Hopefully, you're right and they will." They were both silent a minute, then she touched his hand with hers. Her mouth turned down and her brow creased. "We've just had our first fight. I don't think I liked it."

He pulled her into another embrace. "I guess we did, and I agree. Let's try to avoid them in the future. But, when they happen—and given my bad temper and your stubbornness, I'm sure they will— let's get past them really fast. Okay?" He started to kiss her again when his cell phone rang.

His mouth thinned when he identified the caller. "Llewellyn," he answered. "Yeah, Henry...Oh?...Really?...You're certain?" Looking down at Claire, he frowned. "Well, that's interesting..." He glanced at his watch. "Where is the agency located?...Okay, yeah. We'll meet you there in about twenty or thirty minutes... Thanks again, man."

As he pushed the end button, he pointed to one of the chairs. "Sit down for a second." Luke sat directly across from her. He looked pensive as he filled her in. "That was Henry Kim. You remember the guy I asked to look into your adoption? He had news. He found your foster mother."

She blinked. "*What?* Oh my goodness! What does that mean?"

"Well, for starters, right now we need to hop in a car and head to the adoption agency. Henry gave me directions and I think we can make it before they close at 5:00. He talked to Mrs. Lee. She hasn't heard back from the inquiry to your mother, but she did hear from your foster mother. The problem is, she declined to give the information to Henry, saying she'll only provide it after she talks to you."

Claire stood and pulled on his hand. "What are we waiting for? Let's go!"

Luke obligingly rose, but looked a little concerned. "Don't get too excited yet. It's only a start—just a name and maybe contact information."

"But if we have contact information and she's responded to the adoption agency's query, wouldn't that mean she's willing to see me? To talk to me?"

He considered her question as he opened the door and ushered her through.

"Maybe… Hopefully." His lips turned up slightly and he squeezed her hand. "I guess we'll find out."

THE OFFICES OF the Asia Social Welfare Agency were located in a well-maintained, narrow, four-story building about five miles from Yongsan Garrison. Luke had directions and Claire remembered the area from her previous visit, so they found the agency well within the thirty-minute time frame Luke had set with Henry Kim.

Claire didn't try to hide her excitement as she jogged up the steps to the agency's entrance. She forced herself to wait for Luke to join her, and he smiled as he opened the door.

A middle-aged Korean man was sitting in a small waiting area just inside the entrance. He was relatively thin and his short, coal black hair was brushed back, making no attempt to cover his receding hairline. The creases at the corners of his chocolate-colored eyes suggested friendliness, and he was casually dressed in a black polo shirt and khaki slacks.

During the drive from Yongsan, Luke

told Claire that Henry Kim was Korean-American. He'd been born in the Los Angeles area to Korean immigrants and lived there until age fifteen. His family had returned to Seoul when he was in high school, and Henry spent the next fifteen years moving back and forth between his birth country and his ancestral homeland before finally settling in Seoul. He had multiple computer science degrees from Stanford and UCLA and currently worked for one of the large electronics firms. In his spare time, Henry helped the American military and U.S. State Department with cyber security issues and other classified activities.

Henry Kim was looking at messages on his smartphone when they arrived. When he saw Luke, he immediately closed the app, pocketed the device and rose. Stepping forward, he grinned and held out his hand. "Hey, brother. Good timing."

Luke shook his hand and gave him a friendly thump on his shoulder. "Thanks for getting on this so quickly. I owe you."

He pulled Claire to stand beside him and made the introductions. Claire shook

Henry's hand and said, "I very much appreciate you helping me out like this." She was a little shy. "I'm eager to find out what you've learned."

"Not a problem. I've worked with Luke quite a bit on some of the Army's—um—projects. Happy to help on something personal—and frankly, this easy—for a change." He gave Luke a sly and meaningful look. "Ah, here's Mrs. Lee. She'll walk you through what she's already told me." He glanced again at Luke. "I'll hang around for a while, just in case you need any help translating."

"We'd appreciate it. Thanks." Luke nodded as he turned to meet the woman walking in their direction.

Mrs. Lee was a regal woman of about fifty. She was well dressed in a navy suit, with a pink blouse and low-heeled pumps. Her black hair reached to her chin and was painstakingly coiffed. She greeted Claire with a slight smile and gentle nod. "Miss Olsen. I am glad you could come this afternoon. I have good news."

Claire nodded politely. "Thank you for speaking with Mr. Kim and seeing me this afternoon." She motioned toward Luke. "Let me introduce my good friend. This is Luke Llewellyn from Yongsan." She was a little awkward with the introduction, not really sure how to explain how she came to be in the custody of the naval officer, so she decided to forgo details.

Mrs. Lee made no move to offer her hand, so Luke gave her a brief bow and said, "It's good to meet you, ma'am."

With the introductions made, Mrs. Lee asked the three visitors to accompany her to her office. Although nothing was said to them, the eyes of nearly a dozen women working in cubicles followed the group as they walked to the rear of the building and entered a small office.

Once seated, Henry Kim took over the conversation. "Mrs. Lee, please tell Miss Olsen what you told me about her foster mother."

Mrs. Lee nodded. "Yes, of course." She gave Claire a rather maternal smile. "I do not hear from birth mother—um—yet. I do hear from foster mother." She paused for dramatic effect. "She agree to meet you."

Claire bit her lip and sat up straighter.

"That is wonderful! When did she say we could meet?" It took her a moment to process the news, but she managed, "Can I go see her?"

"Yes, tomorrow, next day… She say is all right." She paused then and said several sentences to Henry in Korean. He asked a question, which she promptly answered.

Henry nodded and turned to Claire and Luke. "Your foster mother's name is Sun Eun-hey. Mrs. Sun lives just outside of a village in the hills, about two hours east of Seoul. It's near some of the big ski areas."

Claire glanced at Luke almost pleadingly. Obviously, this development was unexpected and complicated under the circumstances. She was confined to a military base, had no personal transportation, and no way of finding a woman's home in a rural area two hours out of Seoul.

Luke appeared to read her mind. "I can wrap up some stuff when I go back to work this evening. I'll request a vehicle and we can drive up tomorrow morning." He turned to Henry. "Are you free tomorrow?"

"No, sorry," Henry replied. "I've gotta go to Jeju in the morning."

Luke shrugged. "Not a problem. I'll ask around the base. I'm sure I can find a translator who can go with us."

Claire nearly squeaked. "No, wait! Luke, I forgot! Jessica and Tony had planned on coming for lunch tomorrow. Maybe they can go with us. Jessica can translate. It'll be fun to spend some time with them."

"Sure," Luke said. "Why don't you call Jessica and see if that'll work." He turned back to address Mrs. Lee. "Can you contact Mrs. Sun and inform her that we can be there tomorrow… Say about 1:00?"

"I will do so now. It will take time for call." She gave Claire a meaningful look. "While you wait, would you like to see agency?" She looked pensive then said something to Henry in Korean.

Henry listened and looked at Claire with something akin to compassion. "Mrs. Lee said that you need to see where you spent the first month of your life. She said that it is important to know your heritage—this part of your past."

Claire was simultaneously intrigued and

apprehensive. She glanced at Luke. "Will it be okay to look around the agency? Do you have time before you need to get back?"

He was watching her carefully. His lips turned up in a small smile and his voice was quiet. "Claire, I think it's important for us both to see the agency. Take all the time you want."

Mrs. Lee rose and went to the door of her office. She called to a young woman who was working at a nearby cubicle and motioned her over. After conversing with Mrs. Lee for a moment, the woman smiled shyly and nodded to Claire. "This is Miss Bang," Mrs. Lee said. "She is a case worker. She will show you around and tell you about our agency."

Henry remained seated when Luke and Claire rose. "It's probably a good idea for me to hang around here while Mrs. Lee contacts Mrs. Sun. I'll try to talk to her directly so I can get precise directions. Trying to find a random house in the Korean countryside can be tricky."

Luke nodded. "Good idea. I don't know how long we'll be. So when you get the information, you could send it to me in an email or text and then head out. We've already taken too much of your time." He shook Henry's hand. "And, thanks again."

Leaving Mrs. Lee's office, Claire walked beside Miss Bang and Luke followed closely. Glancing between her guests, Miss Bang said, "My name is Enjie, but call me Katie. Mrs. Lee told me to tell you about our orphanage and show you the dorms and the nursery."

"Your English is very good," Claire said. "Have you spent time in the United States?"

Katie's smile was timid. "No, I studied English here. But after college, I spent one year touring Australia. I lived in several cities, working odd jobs. That helped my English very much." She pushed open the door to an enclosed stairway at the back of the building. "I hope to go to New York and California in a few years."

Katie started the tour with basic information about the agency. "In Korea, we are sometimes called an 'orphanage,' but we are a full-service adoption agency. We are the second largest agency in Korea, and we place about a thousand babies each year."

She led Claire and Luke up the first flight of stairs. "The second floor is meeting rooms and storage. The third floor contains the nursery and the fourth floor is where the mothers stay if they come to Seoul to have their babies." She opened the door and ushered them down the second floor hallway. "As you can see, we have a small conference room on one side and three family rooms for prospective parents and babies on the other."

The family rooms resembled casual living rooms, complete with a small sofa, a few chairs, tables and lamps. The door to one of these rooms was closed and muffled voices and laughter could be heard from beyond. Katie smiled with pleasure. "There is a new family here picking up their baby... It is a very happy time."

She led the way back to the stairs and they went up again. On the landing of the third floor, they found a fairly large bookcase that served as a shoe rack. Katie explained, "The upper floors are considered living areas, therefore we do not wear shoes." Claire and Luke followed Katie's example and removed their shoes before climbing to the next floor in their socks. "We'll go to the dorm first and complete the tour with the babies."

She climbed to the top floor and opened a door leading to a long corridor. "These days," Katie said, "almost all of the babies are adopted by Korean families. That was not always the case. For many years, most of the infants were sent to the United States, Canada or Australia. Now, the babies that are sent away are typically those who Korean parents do not want." She glanced at Claire, but resolutely continued. "Those are the infants that have some health or developmental problems, or those who are not pure—or rather true Korean." She bit her lip and looked away before turning to lead the way down the corridor. There were doors on either side, spaced about fifteen feet apart. Each door had a number, much like a hotel.

"This is only one of our dorms. There are actually six others around the country. The mothers move here right before they deliver. Today there are only five residing in this building."

At the end of the corridor was a large,

airy room that was a combination living room and kitchen. Two pregnant women were sitting in comfortable-looking chairs. One was reading and the other was watching a Korean soap opera on a large flat-screen TV. The women only glanced at Claire and Katie, but they seemed to stare at Luke. Katie nodded to the women but made no move to introduce them to Luke and Claire.

Heading back down the corridor toward the stairs, Claire said, "Tell us a little about the mothers. For example, are they young? Poor? Educated?"

Katie answered without hesitation. "They are mostly between eighteen and twenty-five. We have very few younger than that, which is good. Almost all have finished school and many have at least attended college. None are married."

"Do they ever keep their babies?"

"Yes, at least some do now. It was once very rare, but being a single mother is becoming less of a stigma." She paused in the stairway between the third and fourth floors. "It is difficult—although improving—because of their relationship with their families. It is still shameful and the girls are frequently disowned for dishonoring their family. Unless the mother has a good job, it is difficult for her to afford a child alone."

"What about the fathers?" Luke asked. "Are they ever involved?"

Katie glanced at him. "Sometimes, but it is rare." She looked a little uncomfortable but was candid nonetheless. "Very often, the father of the baby is already married. It is common for working men—those with good jobs and good incomes—to have women in addition to their wives. On some occasions, the father will pay to help the girlfriend to keep the baby. And in rare situations, the father will actually adopt the baby and raise it with his wife. Most of the time, however, the man deserts the woman when she becomes pregnant."

Katie opened the door leading from the stairway into the third floor, effectively changing the subject. "And here is the nursery area." Her voice held obvious pride. "The babies come to us as soon as they are stable—about two or three days, and they stay here until about three or four weeks of age. Then they go to their foster mother until they are six months old. Sometimes if a baby has health problems, we will keep them here longer."

The trio entered a medium-size anteroom in the center of the second floor. On either side were large windows—much like the windows in hospital nurseries—that served to showcase the large rooms housing the babies. Both of the rooms were fairly large, about twenty by thirty feet, and were brightly lit by generous windows with raised blinds.

In the main nursery, Claire saw tallish, rectangular wooden boxes about two feet wide. Pushed up against the wall just under the window, these waist-high structures served as beds for some of the babies. The beds were painted white, with partitions separating the infants. Claire counted four of the beds on the near wall, under the window, and each held four little babies.

The infants were lying on their sides on a padded surface covered by a sheet. They appeared to be identically dressed in white footed pajamas, and were swaddled in white blankets. Only their tiny heads were visible. Most were sleeping, but several were fussing and two could be heard crying, although the sound was muffled by the glass. The perpendicular side of the room held another four beds, and most contained a bundled newborn.

The far side of the room, opposite the window, held cabinets full of baby bottles, cans of powered formula and some medicines. Three women were present. Each was providing some sort of care to an infant. One woman was rocking and feeding a tiny baby; one was giving another a clean diaper; and the third wrapped a baby before laying it in a swing, which she started in motion.

Through a door in the far corner of the room, a small kitchen area was visible, and beyond that was another brightly lit room with a number of baby beds. Women could be seen moving back and forth in those areas, caring for babies there, as well.

Opposite the main nursery, Claire could see two large incubators and several standard baby beds. One caregiver was visible, and about five or six infants were sleeping.

Katie indicated the smaller room. "This

is where we keep the children who need more care. Sometimes we have preemies or infants with a health problem and we move them here to keep them away from the other children." She pointed to the far room, beyond the kitchen area. "In there are the older babies, the ones who will be moving out in the next week or so."

Claire looked over at Luke and saw that he was watching a caregiver in the main room. The woman mixed scoops of powered formula with water taken from a warming container. She filled a bottle, carried it to one of the crying babies and slipped the nipple gently into the tiny mouth. The baby ceased crying immediately and the caregiver propped the bottle on a towel, adjusting it to ensure the baby could suck and swallow easily. She returned to the work table, consulted a different card and repeated the process with another newborn.

"How many babies do you have?" he asked, his voice almost a whisper. He continued to observe the activity in the nursery.

"Normally, we have between thirty and

forty babies here. The most we've had since I started is sixty-two." She shook her head and gave a small sigh. "Too many babies is very hard for the nurses. We have to add help and it is difficult to provide the care they need."

"How do they possibly keep up? I guess each baby has to be fed and changed five or six times a day…and then bathing…"

"Our nurses are experienced and patient," Katie replied. "They take very good care of the children while they are with us."

Claire studied the scene with mixed emotions. The infants were safe and well tended. Their need for warmth, nutrition and cleanliness were met with efficiency and competence. Further, the nurses appeared to be affectionate with the tiny babies, as she witnessed the women talking softly to them and patting them tenderly. But she also saw that much of the care was automatic. The nurses changed so many diapers and prepared so many bottles and comforted so many frantic newborns, that something had to be missing.

She did not have to reflect very long to recognize the absent element was love.

No doubt there had been changes in twenty-five years, but Claire had likely occupied a bed similar to these, surrounded by dozens of other infants being cared for by dedicated but busy women. There would be no kisses on the tiny heads or hands; no singing of lullabies to fussy tots; no one to shed tears or worry about adequate weight gain or a slight temperature or a runny nose. She was inwardly grateful that the babies' time here would be brief. Within a few weeks they would go to a foster home, where she hoped and prayed they would receive more individualized and loving attention. And finally, they would go to a permanent family that she hoped would be as loving and wonderful as her own had been.

Claire managed to ask a few relevant questions and responded appropriately to Katie's comments. But the visit left her shaken, and she was glad when Katie politely told them that the tour was concluded and it was time to return to Mrs. Lee.

Luke seemed to sense Claire's distress.

As they followed Katie to the stairs he squeezed her hand. In a few minutes they rejoined Mrs. Lee and graciously thanked Katie for the tour.

THE COUPLE WAS silent during the drive back to the base. Claire was lost in her musings about beginning life in a small room with dozens of other babies—babies whose mothers—and certainly their fathers—did not want them or could not keep them. The babies were safe and cared for, but how different it was from beginning life with two parents in a loving home. For at least the thousandth time, she said a silent prayer of thanksgiving that Peter and Pamela Olsen had worked so hard to adopt a child from Korea. She would be forever grateful that child had been her.

WHEN THEY REACHED the apartment, Luke stepped aside, allowing Claire to enter first. As soon as the door was shut, he pulled her into a hard, clinging embrace. "I've wanted to hold you like this since we entered the orphanage. I want to make it better; to make up for, well, for your having to start your life there." He looked at her so lovingly that her heart clenched. He smoothed his big hands across her face and his voice deepened. "Thank goodness you were 'unadoptable' by a Korean family, and I'm so thankful for your parents." He paused and took a breath. "Now that I think about it, I'm also thankful to your mentor at Mayo who encouraged you to come here. I'm even grateful to the guys who mugged you—although I'd gladly throw them in jail. I'm just grateful—so very grateful—that you're here with me and you love me as much as I love you." He kissed her then.

Claire stifled a sob as she returned his kiss. "Luke, thank you for taking me today and for understanding. I'm thankful for you! You've helped me, protected me, come after me and sheltered me." She lightly ran her fingers across his lips. Fighting tears, she whispered, "I don't know how I could love you this much, this quickly."

He chuckled. "I don't really care. Just don't stop." He pulled her farther into the apartment and kept his arms around her, holding her tight.

Finally, his arms loosened and he kissed her temple. "Unfortunately, I have to head back to work now." His eyes searched hers. "In the meantime, if you're willing, why don't you go to Bridgette's and collect your stuff and move back into Brad's room." He looked both contrite and expectant. "Since you think I'm cute when I apologize, I need to give you ample opportunity to admire my cuteness. To whit—I was wrong to send you away. I'm sorry."

She rolled her eyes and grinned at him. "How can I resist? Consider me moved back in."

CHAPTER FIFTEEN

BY TEN O'CLOCK the next morning, Luke
and Claire had picked up Tony and Jessica
and the group was headed out of Seoul.
Fortunately, Luke had been able to pro-
cure one of the larger vehicles in the base
fleet, a fairly new Hyundai SUV. In consideration of his size, Tony rode shotgun
in the front passenger seat and Jessica sat
in back with Claire.

Henry Kim had emailed Luke very ex-
plicit directions on how to find Claire's
foster mother's home in the Korean countryside. Following the map and using GPS,
Luke exited the freeway about an hour out
of Seoul and continued on a winding, two-
lane road into the lovely rolling, wooded
mountains that made up the vast part of
the country's interior.

Claire was delighted to spend time with
Jessica, whom she hadn't seen for almost

a week, and to get to know Tony better. The swelling that had marred Jessica's eye and the bruises on her face were mostly gone. What still remained was obscured by skillfully applied makeup. Jessica's right arm was now encased in a hard cast that was suspended by a paisley print silk scarf. She seemed to have put the incident behind her and was as gregarious and outgoing as ever.

Likewise, Tony seemed very much at ease. During the drive through the winding mountain roads, Claire caught him stealing glances at her friend, who never failed to smile back.

"Jessica," Luke said, interrupting one of those grins. "You've heard by now that Claire was born here then adopted to the U.S. We thought you might help us speculate—for lack of a better word—as to whether that might be the reason someone wants to kill her."

Jessica sat up straight, clearly interested. "Actually, I wondered about your ancestry from the beginning." She looked at Claire. "Obviously, you're biracial—Asian and Caucasian—and it just seemed logical that one of your parents was Korean. I had no idea you were actually born *here*." She looked contemplative. "Since you called yesterday I've pondered it a little." She took a breath. "Twenty-five years ago, South Korea was still pulling out of the ashes following the war. It was moving from a third world or developing country to what it is today, behind only China and Japan—economically speaking—in Asia. But at that time, the country was very conservative socially. It still is, but it was even more so back then. Out-of-wedlock pregnancies were quite scandalous." She looked sympathetically at Claire and then explained. "It would have been particularly shameful, however, if the baby had not been a pure-blood Korean. In other words, giving birth to a mixed-race baby would be a dishonor beyond redemption."

"Okay, so you think Claire's heritage—that her father was Caucasian—would have been this huge disgrace?" Tony said and then frowned. "But that was then… Baby got born. Baby got adopted. Twenty-five years pass…" He shrugged. "Why would someone care now?"

"Well obviously someone does—big-time," Luke said.

Jessica looked pensive for a while. "The only thing I can think of—and this really is pure speculation—is that the woman who got pregnant and/or Claire's father was someone of note."

"How so?" asked Claire.

"Well, if your birth mother was in one of the higher social classes, she'd need to hide having a mixed-race baby. Depending on who she was, it might be necessary to keep the secret forever. My guess would be for position or money or both." Jessica frowned. "You know, at that time, the only Korean women who would've had any interaction with non-Korean men would be the very wealthy and influential—like heads of industry, those in government, diplomats or maybe actresses—or the very lower class." She bit her lip and looked at Claire. "Like a prostitute…"

"I wondered about that," Luke said. "But who would care if the child of a prostitute returned to the country twenty-five years later?"

"I guess in that case, the focus would

be on the father... Who was *he?*" Jessica frowned. "I think that scenario is much more far-fetched, because twenty-five years later, any diplomat or high-level military officer would be long gone and would have no way of knowing, even if he did care."

"You're right," Claire said. "That doesn't make sense... So, if we are to believe that something about my heritage is driving the attempts to um...harm me, then the reason probably has to do with who my mother is, or, more accurately, who her parents are."

"Hopefully, your foster mother can give us some answers," Luke said.

ACCORDING TO THE INFORMATION Henry had gathered, Mrs. Sun lived on a small farm that grew fruit—strawberries and peaches—and ginseng.

They arrived a little before one o'clock at the traditionally styled Korean farmhouse. The lovely structure was built from bleached wood, complete with a blue tiled roof and gently curving eaves. After considerable discussion they agreed that Jessica and Claire would approach the house and the men would remain in the SUV until they had Mrs. Sun's permission to enter. Neither Luke nor Tony wanted to frighten the woman, who was likely in her sixties or seventies.

Claire's heart rate was high when she knocked on the door. It was immediately opened by a middle-aged woman with a dour expression, wearing the black skirt and white blouse of a maid. Jessica introduced herself and Claire, and politely asked for Mrs. Sun. The maid seemed curious about the blonde woman's excellent command of Korean and the Korean woman with the odd eyes. After a short pause she mumbled something and stepped aside, allowing them to enter.

The women slipped off their shoes, placed them on a rack just inside the door and followed the maid into the house. Jessica turned to Claire and said quietly, "She said that Mrs. Sun is expecting us."

In only a few steps they were admitted to a bright and airy room, which had wide, open windows. It was nicely appointed and the furnishings and art appeared expensive. A petite, white-haired woman was sitting on a low stool when Jessica and Claire entered.

Jessica placed her hand on Claire's forearm, stopping her progress. "Wait just a second," she instructed under her breath. "Give her a small bow."

Claire smiled tentatively to the woman, then bowed, as instructed. *"Anyong haseyo,"* she said politely.

Mrs. Lee rose to her feet. Claire realized at once that she was quite stooped with osteoporosis, but she stood as straight as she could and regally walked across the room to stop in front of Claire. Her face was serious but curious as she stared at Claire for what seemed like a long time. Finally she said something. At first the words sounded harsh, but then she smiled, reached up and touched her gently on the cheek.

Jessica smiled slightly and was forced to blink back threatening tears. "She commented on your eyes—she said the family called them 'bad eyes.' And then she called you 'my baby'."

Claire felt her own eyes become damp and she swallowed hard. Finally she was able to smile at the elderly woman and she said, "Thank you, Mrs. Sun, for taking care of me. I am happy to meet you now."

She waited for Jessica to translate and she watched the old woman smile. She touched her cheek again and then she caught Claire's hand and pulled her toward the low table in the center of the room. She said some words that Jessica translated. "She wants us to have tea."

"Should we ask to include Luke and Tony?"

"Okay, but I'll introduce them as our husbands," she whispered under her breath. She relayed the information to the older woman and pointed toward the door.

Mrs. Sun looked pleased and then clapped her hands, calling for the maid. She sent her to fetch the two men, and they joined the tea party only a few minutes later, minus their shoes. The living room seemed to shrink with the arrival of the two big men, who bowed respectfully and graciously thanked the elderly woman for her hospitality.

The serving of tea and polite words followed. After everyone had finished at least one cup, Jessica finally broached the reason for their visit. She asked Mrs. Sun to tell Claire what she knew about her birth mother.

The old woman said something but was interrupted by Jessica. It was obvious that what she'd said was a surprise. Jessica asked another question, was answered, and then she sat up straighter and turned to Claire. She took a deep breath and explained. "Well, this is already interesting. It seems that Mrs. Sun is actually your great aunt. She is your grandmother's sister."

Claire was a little flustered by that revelation. "Oh, I'm not sure how to respond… I guess tell her that's wonderful." She managed a smile at the older woman and tears formed in her eyes once more.

Jessica translated and asked another question. The back-and-forth continued for some time. Claire or occasionally Luke would ask questions, Jessica would interpret, Mrs. Sun would answer, and Jessica would interpret again.

In the end, Mrs. Sun was very informative. She told them Claire's mother was Lee Won-ji, a privileged, wealthy young woman who was twenty when Claire was born. Mrs. Sun was not complimentary with regard to the young woman. At one point Jessica looked at Claire and behind her to Luke and Tony and said, "Mrs. Sun said that she—Claire's mother—was a stupid, selfish, greedy—well, um, she actually used a derogatory word… I think she didn't approve of her. Also, interestingly, she lived here with Mrs. Sun during the pregnancy, which is how Mrs. Sun came to be your foster mother."

Claire nodded. Then her brow creased with a slight frown. "Where is she now?"

Jessica asked the question and waited for the answer. When it came she bit her lip before turning to tell Claire. "Well, she said your birth mother died only a couple of years after you were born. She was only twenty-three. I'm sorry."

Claire wasn't sure what she'd been expecting, but that news was somehow stunning. Finally she managed to say, "I'm sorry, too. What happened?" Her voice was quiet, and tears created twin tracks, dampening her cheeks.

Following Jessica's translation of the

question, Mrs. Sun again seemed disapproving. Jessica looked pained when she repeated what had been said. "Uh, well, she was driving her car and had an accident. It seems she was—er—she'd had too much *soju*." Jessica looked uncomfortable describing the young woman's intake of alcohol. "Apparently, after your birth, she became very much a 'party girl' and, well...she killed herself in the accident."

They all took a few moments to digest that revelation and Mrs. Sun said something. Jessica nodded and explained. "Won-ji's parents are also dead. Her mother—Mrs. Sun's sister—died only last year. Her father died about five years ago from liver cancer."

Claire realized that with the exception of this great aunt, her Korean family members might all be dead. But what about her father? She caught Jessica's eye. "Ask her if she knows anything about my father?"

Jessica complied and waited a span while the old woman went into a fairly lengthy oration.

"Hmm...Well, okay." She gave Claire another concerned look, fortifying herself before sharing what she'd learned. "When she was staying here during her pregnancy, your mother eventually confided in Mrs. Sun that she met a very handsome man at the yearly American Embassy Ball. Your father was a career diplomat and the primary assistant to the American ambassador at that time. Evidently, he was fluent in Korean and was able to easily seduce your mother with promises of marriage. According to Mrs. Sun, it was all a lie, because when Won-ji informed him of her pregnancy, he confessed he was married and had three children in California. It seems he pretty much told her to 'get lost' and left Korea shortly thereafter. She never heard from him again."

Claire felt pity for the young woman, suddenly finding herself pregnant by the poor excuse for a man who was evidently her father. Once again she breathed a sigh of relief to have been adopted by loving, stable parents. She was also glad that she hadn't previously known about the uncomfortable circumstances surrounding her conception and birth. She almost wished she didn't know now. But that reality didn't change who she was. She straightened her spine and silently said another prayer of thanks.

Everyone was silent for a few minutes as they considered the latest revelations. It was Luke who asked the most pressing question. His voice was edgy and his anger was subdued, but evident to the Americans. "Jessica, ask her who from the family is still alive. Who would benefit from Claire's death?"

Jessica carefully considered how to phrase Luke's question, then relayed it to Mrs. Sun. The old woman sat still for a moment, evidently contemplating how much to divulge.

When she didn't immediately reply, Luke repeated the question. "Who would benefit from Claire's death?" His attention turned from Jessica to Mrs. Sun. Evidently his bitterness needed no translation and Mrs. Sun suddenly seemed more afraid of Luke than she was apprehensive about disclosing potentially damaging information. She finally answered. Her words were softer and spoken more hesitantly than before, but her confidence seemed to increase as she provided the information.

Jessica translated.

"His name is Lee Min-sik. He is your birth mother's only brother. Evidently he inherited all the family money—which according to Mrs. Sun was considerable." She paused and glanced at Mrs. Sun. "He also inherited his father's position. The elder Mr. Lee was part of the founding group of a Korean conglomerate—kind of like Samsung and LG. It seems that he's now—"

Mrs. Sun interrupted her, saying something under her breath that caused Jessica to pause. Stunned, the blonde sat up straight and turned to Claire. "Mrs. Sun thinks Mr. Lee actually brought about your mother's death—because of you. He encouraged her drinking and allowed her to drive even though she was inexperienced. He hated the shame that she brought on the family because her baby was not Korean."

Mrs. Sun said a few more words that seemed sorrowful and these, too, Jessica translated. "She said to tell you that she is sorry, but Mr. Lee thought you were the 'highest disgrace'—that is the term she used—to the family. He believed you should not be allowed to live."

CHAPTER SIXTEEN

THE CONVERSATION WAS subdued as they drove back down the curving, narrow road toward the highway. As before, Jessica and Claire were in the back of the SUV, with Tony beside Luke. After about fifteen minutes, Jessica patted Claire on the arm. "That was a lot to take in. Are you doing okay?"

Claire managed a small smile. "Yes, actually, I'm fine. More than anything, it's a relief to know who wants to harm me and why. I'll never know more about my birth father, but that's okay. I don't think I would've liked him… Mostly, I feel sorry for my birth mother, and I guess for her parents. Honestly I'm thankful for how it turned out… Not about them, of course, but that I was adopted by wonderful parents."

"What's the next step?" asked Tony.

"As soon as we get back to Seoul, I'm going to drop you and Jessica off and take Claire to see Captain Choi. He'll be able to take it from here with regard to dear Uncle Lee. I also want to get your passport released." He glanced in the rearview mirror to catch Claire's eye. "It's time for you to go home." His words were soft and authoritative.

She nodded. "Yes. I agree. I think I want to go home." A single tear slid down her cheek. "I'm a little overwhelmed right now and home is a good place to be." Jessica reached over to squeeze her hand. Suddenly fatigued, Claire leaned back and closed her eyes.

THE QUARTET WAS SILENT for the next several miles, everyone focused on their own thoughts. Without warning, Luke looked askance at Tony and said, "Are you carrying?" His voice was low and without inflection.

"Yes." Tony glanced at Luke then turned to study the road behind them. He spied a single car about a quarter of a mile behind the SUV. "Is there a problem?"

"Yeah. Looks like. Two guys in that black sedan. I've been varying my speed quite a bit; they are definitely copying me." He slowly increased speed until the rate was bordering on dangerous.

As Tony watched, the sedan's speed increased proportionately. Avoiding sudden moves that might alarm Jessica and Claire, he reached behind his back and pulled out his 9 mm automatic pistol. The weapon was actually illegal in Korea, but an exception was granted for American Embassy security officers, including Tony.

Although Luke maintained his speed on the narrow, winding mountain road, the black sedan seemed to be gaining. Luke drove another mile and when they hit a straight spot in the road, he braked, slowing the SUV by almost twenty miles per hour. The sedan roared up fairly close and Luke pulled toward the shoulder, ostensibly offering to let the sedan pass. It didn't. Luke slowed even more and the sedan nearly stopped, staying about 150 feet behind.

"Claire, Jessica." Luke's voice was a

bit louder, but his words remained calm. "Make sure your seat belts are tight."

Jessica had been reading a journal and Claire had been dozing, but both immediately become attentive. "What's wrong?" Jessica asked.

"I think we have company. Check your seatbelt. You, too, Claire."

Both women followed his instructions. "Oh, God, not again!" Claire glanced back and saw the car. Her voice held fear and frustration. "How? I don't understand!"

Luke caught her eye in the rearview mirror. "The only thing I can think of is that they must have been staking out Mrs. Sun's. Obviously, they're very determined."

He pressed the accelerator and had the vehicle up to seventy in a few seconds. The sedan was quickly gaining on them again, this time inching even closer.

"Whaddya think?" Tony asked. "Want me to try taking out a tire?"

"Let's wait to see if they actually make a move." Luke sped up a little more, carefully watching the road in front of them and the car behind.

Tony unfastened his seatbelt and turned around facing the rear, kneeling on his seat. He cradled the big pistol in both hands, pointing it to the ceiling. Jessica gasped when she saw the weapon. "You think you're going to need that?" Her voice was pitched high and a little tremulous.

"Don't know," he answered without taking his eyes from the car. "Hope not."

Even as he spoke, the black sedan roared forward, pulling up only a few feet from the SUV's bumper. They rode that way for about half a mile and then, as they were approaching a curve, the sedan's driver increased his speed. The vehicle swerved and pulled up beside them, but still about half a car length behind. Safely able to make the move, Luke slammed on the brakes and the sedan shot ahead. The driver reacted immediately, though, braking and swerving into an abrupt "U" turn. Both vehicles came to a complete stop, now facing each other.

Unfortunately, the SUV was at an outside curve. Therefore Luke was unable to reverse without taking a horrible chance of backing into someone coming around the winding hill. Luke nodded to Tony who was again facing forward. Tony opened his window, and pointed the gun toward the oncoming car.

"Ladies, get down *now*." Luke's voice was still calm but commanding. Immediately, Claire and Jessica complied, leaning forward as much as their seatbelts allowed.

Staring straight ahead, Luke said, "Let's go." He hit the gas, punching the SUV forward. Simultaneously, Tony leaned out his window and aimed for the sedan's tires. He fired three shots in quick succession as the SUV came dangerously near the stopped sedan. Luke barely slowed as they swerved, narrowly avoiding a sideswipe. As they roared by, Tony leaned out and fired two more shots, this time aiming at the car's rear tires.

"Hit anything?" Amazingly, Luke's voice was still emotionless.

"Hard to tell. At least they know we have a weapon. That might be a deterrent." Tony kept his voice calm. They could have been discussing the weather.

"Doesn't look like it." Luke's voice grew marginally edgier. "Here they come."

Tony swore under his breath. He turned again and saw that the sedan was only a few feet behind them. Even though Luke increased his speed, they were jolted as the sedan hit their rear bumper.

Tony glanced down at the women. "Jessica, Claire, keep your heads down and cover them with your arms. I'm going to blow out the window." The next blast punched through the rear window, showering the two women with tiny bits of glass. Unfortunately, the safety glass was hearty, and about two-thirds of the fractured window remained in place, blocking Luke and Tony's view of the black sedan.

Tony swore loudly. He glanced at Luke, who was now forced to rely on his side mirrors. "Can you see well enough to keep up with them?"

"Yeah. I got it." Luke sped up once again, edging dangerously fast for the winding road. "It looks like a tire is out, but that doesn't seem to be slowing them much. It will eventually, but you might try to get a shot in the engine block. If that doesn't work, go for the driver."

Tony deftly crawled over the console

and wedged himself between Claire and Jessica. With the barrel of his weapon, he cleared away enough of the shattered window to see the target. He propped the pistol on the top of the seat and fired two more shots. The bullets hit the front of the sedan, but it was difficult to tell if anything vital was damaged.

Despite, or perhaps because of, the shredding tire and the probable engine damage, the sedan's driver became even more reckless. He slammed down the accelerator and rear-ended the SUV, sending Tony sprawling backward onto the console between the two front seats. The jolt nearly caused Luke to lose control, but he managed to avoid hitting the side of the hill to their right.

While Luke fought to maintain control, Tony crawled back to his seat. He crouched sideways, with the pistol aimed toward the driver's side window, hoping to get off a shot at the sedan's driver. Within seconds, the black car sped forward and rammed them just as they rounded a curve. Suddenly both vehicles were careening down the hill. Luke hit the brakes and tried desperately to keep the SUV from rolling, while fighting to dodge trees. The passengers were subjected to horribly deafening screeching and grinding noises as the sides and undercarriage of the vehicle were scraped by branches. As they were sliding to a stop, the vehicle hit a loose bit of gravel, causing a skid which ended as they slammed almost head-on into a tree.

LUKE'S EARS RANG with screams from the backseat, loud bursts that sounded like shotgun blasts, the shattering of the windshield and the crumpling of the SUV's frame. The cacophony of sounds ceased as abruptly as the vehicle came to a stop, and there followed a sudden and almost eerie quiet.

When the airbag deployed, Luke was hit hard in the face and chest. A few seconds passed before he could catch his breath.

Luke shuddered, trying to focus. As his mind cleared, he unbuckled his seatbelt and turned to the backseat. "Claire!" His voice was ripe with dread. "Claire, are you okay?" Both women were still leaning forward, their heads covered by their hands.

At his urgent questioning, both hesitantly sat up and looked around.

"Luke, there's smoke!" Claire cried as she fumbled to undo her seatbelt.

Jessica managed to unlatch hers and struggled to push open her door. "I can't open it!"

"No, it's okay. It's not smoke." Luke tried to calm them. "It's powder from the airbags. It's not smoke."

Luke was immensely relieved that Claire and Jessica appeared to be unharmed. His relief was short-lived, however, when he turned to Tony. The marine was slumped sideways, with his head partially out of the now broken side window.

As Luke had struggled to control their crash, he'd been dimly aware that Tony was trying to brace himself by holding on to the dash with one hand and his seat with the other. But the front passenger side had sustained the worst damage from hitting the tree. And Tony hadn't been wearing his seatbelt. His momentum had thrust him back toward the door then the airbags deployed, which pushed him hard into the seat before they deflated, causing him to fall to one side.

In the crowded confines of the totaled vehicle, Luke managed to hoist himself up and lean over to gently pull Tony back into a semi sitting position. A quick assessment revealed a deep, two-inch laceration in his forehead, neatly dissecting his right eyebrow, along with multiple smaller cuts dotting the side of his face. The deep cut was bleeding profusely, and Luke pressed hard with two fingers, trying to stop the flow. "Do either of you have something we can use for a pressure bandage?" he barked.

"Here, let me help," Claire said.

CLAIRE SCRAMBLED to get as close as she could, leaning over the back of Tony's seat. She held the injured man's head while Jessica rifled through her purse and came up with a wad of Kleenex. She handed the tissues to Claire who pressed them hard against the wound.

"Give me that scarf." Luke motioned to Jessica's sling. She handed it to him and he quickly ripped it in half, tying both ends together to make a bandage. While Claire held the tissues in place, she palpated Tony's throat, locating his carotid artery. Although his pulse was a little rapid, it was strong.

Claire held Tony's head steady while Luke wrapped it with the makeshift bandage. When that had been accomplished, Luke said, "We need to get away from here. I don't know if they survived the crash, but they may be on their way now." Although the driver's side door was partially caved in by the crash, Luke was able to force it open, subjecting the group to another grinding screech of metal on metal. Claire's door had not been affected. She opened it and both women clambered out. Luke took precious seconds to scan the hill behind them where the black sedan had also crashed down. From their spot amid trees and other brush, he couldn't see the other vehicle and didn't pick up any movement.

He looked at Claire. "I'm going to have to pull Tony out. I need you to crawl in and try to guide his legs."

She gave a brief nod and then climbed through the driver's seat and carefully edged over Tony, pressing her back against the door. As she did, she spotted Tony's handgun on the floorboard. "Luke, here." She handed him the weapon. He took it and then shoved it toward Jessica, who was standing next to him, anxiously watching their efforts and looking around for the men who'd run them off the road.

Luke knelt on the driver's seat and reached behind Tony's back, grasping him under the arms. He pulled gently, but steadily backward, cradling his head. From her spot, Claire was able to help lift his legs over the console. As she did, she was surprised by how heavy they were. Although Luke controlled the bulk of Tony's weight, Claire struggled to help him through the door. In only a few moments, they had extracted the injured man from the SUV, and Luke laid him carefully on the ground.

He looked at Claire. "Can you check him to see if there's anything broken? If he has a spinal cord injury, we've probably done him additional harm, but that can't be helped. We have to get out of here."

Claire got on her knees and performed a

quick assessment. She didn't find any obvious broken bones and she lifted both eyelids and whispered a prayer of thanks that his pupils were equal and reacted evenly, constricting quickly when exposed to the sunlight. Some blood had seeped through the Kleenex and stained Jessica's torn scarf, but the flow seemed to have nearly stopped. His pulse was still strong, but he didn't show signs of regaining consciousness.

"I don't see anything glaring, but we need to get him to a hospital as soon as possible." She looked around in despair. They were at least an hour from the outskirts of Seoul in a remote, mountainous area, several hundred yards off the road. Worse, for all they knew, the men who had tried to kill them were still nearby. She couldn't fathom how they would be able to get Tony to a hospital quickly without divine intervention.

She said a quick prayer.

Because she'd been occupied with assessing Tony, Claire didn't know that Luke had pulled out his cell phone until she realized he was talking with someone.

"Yes, it's an emergency...We have a man down..." He proceeded to explain the circumstances and describe Tony's injuries and the terrain. "Got it. About a mile and a half?...I'll relocate the group...I hope about thirty minutes...Yeah...I'm going to give the phone to my colleague so I can carry Sergeant Mancini. Give her the instructions."

Luke handed Claire his phone. "This is Corporal Nunez. He's going to tell us where to go so a helicopter can pick us up."

Claire responded with a tiny nod. "Okay."

With that he squatted down, picked up Tony almost like a baby, then stood. When he was completely erect, he shifted Tony's limp body carefully until he was resting across both shoulders in what Claire recognized as the fireman's carry. Tony was far from a small man, and she estimated that he weighed at least two hundred pounds. The move was done—while not effortlessly—with astonishing ease. Claire glanced at Jessica and both gaped at Luke's display of strength.

The man on the phone regained their attention when he said, "Ma'am, you need to head southwest, farther down the hill, for about 400 yards, then walk across the valley for about half a mile."

"Thank you, Corporal," she managed to reply. "He said we need to go southwest, down the hill... Luke, which way is southwest?"

He actually chuckled and started forward. "Follow me."

Luke led the way with Jessica and Claire following closely behind. Although Claire knew Luke was strong, nonetheless, she was amazed by his stamina as they traversed the uneven terrain. Claire spoke to Corporal Nunez regularly. Without knowing the source of his information, she determined that he had access to some type of topographical program and a GPS system that allowed him to track their exact location.

As they continued their trek through the woods, Claire grew increasingly concerned about Luke. With each step, he seemed to be breathing more rapidly and their pace was slowing. She wanted to help him, but knew there was nothing she and Jessica could do.

They had covered about a mile when Luke said, "I need a break." With that declaration he sank to his knees and sat back on his heels to rest. He didn't move Tony; rather he kept the unconscious man draped across his shoulders. Claire was alarmed by his heavy sweating and rapid breathing. Could he keep moving over the grueling ground while carrying the heavy burden? She didn't know what choice they had.

"Claire, can you check on Tony. See if there's any change?" His voice sounded strained.

Claire dropped to her knees behind Luke and examined Tony as best she could. There was some oozing from the small cuts, but otherwise she didn't detect any change. His hands were warm, his pulse strong and his pupils reactive. "He seems stable." She looked at Luke worriedly. "How are you holding up?"

"I'm okay. I don't think it's a whole lot farther." He managed a slight smile, trying to lessen her concern.

Jessica had been diligently watching their rear. Suddenly, she knelt beside Claire and caught Luke's eye. "Hey, guys, I think I heard a noise. There may be someone following us." She kept her voice low.

Luke managed to turn around to study the woods they had just traversed. All three watched closely for a moment. "Where is Tony's gun?" he asked.

"In my purse." Jessica pointed to her cross-body bag, which she was now using as a sling.

"Get it out." Luke's voice was low. She nodded and complied. "You know how to shoot?" He was still watching the woods.

"I've done a little target work. I can manage."

"Good. Keep it handy. This is making me nervous." He struggled for only a heartbeat as he stood and resolutely started walking. His voice was tense when he glanced at Claire and said, "Ask the corporal for an ETA of the Huey."

Claire relayed the question and was told to expect the helicopter in about twenty minutes. They walked about ten minutes more, but their pace had slowed considerably. Fortunately, the woods seemed to be thinning, which made the path a little easier for Luke to manage.

Jessica remained a few steps behind, watching and listening. Suddenly she cried out, "Stop! *Meom-chweo!*"

Claire and Luke whirled around as Jessica raised the pistol and fired two rounds. There was a sound of thrashing, followed a moment later by quick movements that grew increasingly faint.

"What did you see?" Luke asked.

Jessica gripped the pistol; it wobbled slightly. She kept looking toward the trees. "Mostly just movement of the brush and grass, but a couple of times I thought I saw something black—probably clothing."

"Good going. I think—I hope—that you scared them off… At least for now."

Fatigue etched Luke's face and he struggled with every step. *Please,* she prayed silently, *let us get there quickly.* Into Luke's phone she said, "Corporal, it appears we're being followed. Can you give us an update on how much farther?"

"Huey's less than two minutes from your present location," Corporal Nunez responded. "You're probably five to ten from the rendezvous site." Much relieved, Claire relayed the information to Luke.

"Here, hand me the phone," Luke said. When she complied he said gruffly, "Nunez, request that the Huey do a low flyover of the woods immediately south of our present location...Great... thanks... Giving you back to Ms. Olsen." He handed the phone back to Claire and resumed his pace, moving resolutely toward their goal.

Less than two minutes passed before they heard the helicopter. Another minute and they could see it coming in their direction. It passed immediately overhead and proceeded to do several low sweeps of the area, only a hundred or so feet above the tops of the trees.

Luke chuckled. "That should give them something to think about."

Claire swallowed and nodded. She hoped so; it certainly intimidated her.

The helicopter seemed to follow them for the next five minutes, still doing occasional low forays behind the small group. Its presence, and the assurance that the rendezvous site was near, seemed to bolster Luke's strength. Finally, just as the corporal had predicted, they arrived at a wide clearing. The helicopter flew past them, did a quick circle and sat gracefully down. The roar of the aircraft was deafening as the rotors continued to move.

Luke sank to his knees much as he had before. This time he leaned to one side and eased Tony to the ground. While he was accomplishing that maneuver, two men in olive drab coveralls carrying a collapsible stretcher hopped out of the aircraft, leaving the side doors open wide.

"We've got him, sir," one of the men said, as Luke struggled to move Tony into a more natural position. In quick, practiced moves, the men placed Tony on his back on the stretcher then carried him to the Huey.

Even though he'd been relieved of considerable weight, Luke suddenly seemed weak. Claire and Jessica helped him to his feet and steadied him as he staggered toward the waiting copter.

It took only three minutes to load all four Americans, and shortly thereafter they were airborne.

CHAPTER SEVENTEEN

THE FLIGHT BACK to Yongsan took less than forty minutes. During that time, Claire learned that the helicopter was routinely used for medical evacuations. One of the men who'd carried the stretcher was a medic—Corpsman Sandy Jefferson. Corpsman Jefferson knelt by Tony and quickly and efficiently stabilized his cervical spine by placing a collar around his neck and taping his forehead to the stretcher. When that was accomplished, he took Tony's pulse and blood pressure and completed a check of his neurological system. While Jefferson was conducting his assessment, Claire started an IV.

Jessica watched their ministrations with concern. "Do you think he's going to be okay?" Worry etched her expressive face.

Jefferson responded matter-of-factly. "Don't know if the spinal cord stabilization measures will do any good at this point. But it could help… Not sure about the head injury, but I don't see a lot of the really concerning signs."

Claire tried to be more encouraging. She gave Jessica a smile and said, "Hopefully, he's just concussed and will be coming out of it shortly." She glanced down at the unconscious man and added, "We should know more soon."

After doing as much as possible for Tony, Claire turned her attention to Luke. She was surprised and alarmed when she discovered him slumped in his seat with his eyes closed. He was still sweating heavily and his breathing seemed to be labored. Leaving Tony with the corpsman and Jessica, she edged across the confined space to where he was resting.

She put her hand lightly on his forehead and quietly asked, "Luke, are you all right?" He jerked slightly as if startled and opened his eyes. "I'm sorry. I didn't know you were asleep. I wanted to check on you, too."

Luke appeared to be puzzled by her comment and he stared at her a minute.

"How's Tony?" he asked. His voice was low and he sounded hoarse.

She took his hand; her lips thinned in a slight frown. "He hasn't shown any signs of waking and he hasn't moved yet. But the corpsman said he doesn't see signs of either spinal cord injury or a severe head injury."

He nodded and continued to stare at her. "Where are your glasses?" He sounded tired.

She automatically touched her face and found that sometime during the past hour she'd lost her glasses. Her lips turned up at the corners and she gently clasped his hand. "I've no idea… Are you all right?" she repeated.

"Yeah. Pretty much." He gave her a weak smile and moved slightly, as if adjusting his weight to get more comfortable. "I probably need to be checked out when we get to the hospital." He closed his eyes and whispered, "I like you without the glasses… Of course, I also like you with glasses…"

"Luke, talk to me." Claire rose to her feet, hovering over him. "What's wrong?"

"Ribs." He didn't open his eyes. "I hope they're not broken. I hate broken ribs." His voice was even weaker.

"Which side? Luke, where are you hurt?" She tugged at his shirt, exposing his abdomen and chest. She stifled a gasp when she saw the ugly bruise on his right side. She turned to the medic who was taking Tony's blood pressure for the second time. "Corpsman, when you finish there, can you come check the lieutenant?" She tried not to sound panicked.

Jefferson glanced at Luke's sweaty, pale face. "Sure." He was at her side in a breath. "Whoa, man!…er, sir," he exclaimed. A huge, darkened area covered much of Luke's chest. Jefferson gave Claire a wry look. "They're at least cracked, maybe broken. Probably caused by the steering wheel or the airbag." He took out his stethoscope and listened to the sound of air moving in Luke's right lung. "Sound's okay. A little diminished perhaps, but that may be because his breathing is shallow; most likely he's avoiding deep breaths due to pain." He frowned and shook his head as he wound up the stethoscope and thrust it into his pocket. "Not a lot we can do here—actually there's not much they can do at the hospital, either." He gave Luke a look of admiration. "Don't know how he carried the sergeant that far with those ribs."

Luke opened his eyes and frowned. "Don't talk about me like I'm not here." He rolled his eyes—and groaned, "I *hate* broken ribs."

Claire took his hand and managed a smile. "Have you had much experience with them?"

He nodded and squeezed her hand. His lips thinned as he answered, "Yeah. Football injury. One season I had to play every game with my chest wrapped with this big brace—kind of like Kevlar..." He fell asleep with Claire still holding his hand.

The next several hours were a blur. The Huey landed on the roof of Yongsan Base's hospital. A crew was waiting to rush Tony into the Emergency Department.

Luke's short nap revived him a bit, and he balked when the hospital's medic insisted on putting him in a wheelchair to transport him from the helipad to the E.D.

"I can walk," Luke growled at the young

private who held the wheelchair in place, waiting for him to comply.

Despite his pale face and obvious pain, Luke was still an imposing figure. To the private's credit, however, he didn't flinch. "Hospital policy, sir. You need to sit down and let me push you before I have to call for some help and we strap you in." Only a little anxiety appeared in the young man's expression, but he swallowed hard with relief as Luke obligingly, but with bad grace, took a seat.

Claire and Jessica initially argued when the medical personnel insisted on checking them out, but within a few minutes of landing, all four were in separate cubicles in the well-equipped and well-staffed E.D. Claire was in the best shape, and the nurse practitioner quickly deemed her "good to go," after a thorough assessment.

Because of Jessica's recent hospitalization, the doctor insisted on another X-ray of her fractured arm, and he did a detailed examination of her still bruised face. They found nothing new and nothing of concern so she, too, was discharged within an hour. She joined Claire, who was pacing in the waiting room, eager for details on the condition of Luke and Tony.

Even though hospital personnel were friendly, considerate and professional, they wouldn't let the women see Luke or Tony. Both men, they were told, had been taken for X-rays. The staff were unwilling to discuss the patients, and shared nothing about their status.

Unfortunately, Bridgette was not on duty when they arrived, and Claire asked the admitting clerk to call her friend to tell her about the accident. In less than fifteen minutes, Bridgette barged into the waiting area seeking Claire, eager to provide moral support and act as an information source.

Claire introduced Jessica and Bridgette. Bridgette took one look at the two now exhausted and almost frantic women and said, "Why don't you go to my apartment and rest? I can call you as soon as Tony and Luke are situated somewhere where you can see them."

Claire shook her head adamantly. "No. I'm not leaving. I can't leave them!" The events of the day suddenly crashed down on her and she collapsed into a chair.

Tears stained her face. "This is my fault," she cried. She looked plaintively at Jessica and said, "First it was you—you were hurt." She turned her attention to Bridgette and continued, "And then you could have been..." She bit her lip. "And now Tony and Luke are hurt." She tried in vain to stifle her sobs. "I know Luke's going to be okay, but Tony? Please, God, let Tony be okay!" She doubled over and buried her face in her hands.

Bridgette and Jessica looked at each other, unsure how to appease Claire's grief and guilt. Finally, Jessica put her arm around her friend. "Claire, that's enough. You heard what Mrs. Sun said about your uncle." She shook her head with vehemence. "You didn't cause any of it. You had no control over his actions! You can't blame yourself for what some greedy, maladjusted egomaniac—who you didn't even know existed—does."

Bridgette glanced around the waiting area and located a box of tissues. She handed it to Claire, who gratefully took a couple and whispered, "Thanks." She sighed as she wiped her eyes. "I know, but

I'm still responsible. Tony, Luke…" She waved her hand in a gesture of inclusion and continued, "both of you—you all were only bystanders; only trying to help me."

Bridgette followed Jessica's lead and hugged her friend. Finally, the support of both women helped calm Claire's emotional battle. When her tears had subsided, she looked at her friends and muttered, "I need to call the police." She picked up her purse but then gave a rueful laugh and threw up her hands. Shaking her head, she said, "I don't have a cell phone…"

In the end, Jessica contacted Detective Kang. She was told that he and Captain Choi would be at the hospital within the hour to interview them.

While they were waiting for the police, Bridgette disappeared for a few minutes and returned with two cups of coffee. "You two stay here for a minute. I'm going to see what I can find out about Luke and Tony; I'll be right back."

She was smiling when she returned a short time later. "Okay, Claire, you can come with me. Luke's back from X-ray. He's fine—just cracked ribs. They've admitted him overnight for observation, though, so he's grumpy as all get out and scaring the snot out of the aides and nurses. Maybe you can help calm him."

"What about Tony?" Claire asked.

Bridgette smiled again. "He's coming around. He's not yet completely conscious, but he is moving—and importantly, he's moving all four limbs. There doesn't seem to be any spinal cord damage—which is great news. They stitched up the big cut on his forehead and did some other work on his face." She frowned. "I think they're worried about his right eye, though. There may be a retina issue, but they need him alert to evaluate that better."

Both women were ecstatic with Bridgette's report. Jessica squeezed Claire's hand. "Go check on Luke. I'll stay here and wait on the police. We'll come find you."

Claire followed Bridgette to the third floor. They walked down a couple of corridors and Bridgette knocked loudly at a door before barging in without waiting for a response.

Suddenly hesitant, Claire stayed behind,

hovering at the entrance. Luke was sitting up in a hospital bed, covered to above his waist with a sheet. He was bare-chested, with a wide, bulky dressing wound around his ribcage. He was connected to a heart monitor and an intravenous line was dripping clear fluid into his left hand.

"Hey there," Bridgette said cheerfully as she approached the bed. "Heard you're going to get to stay with us overnight,"

Luke glared at her. "This is stupid. I'm fine. I need to go check on Tony." He raised his arm and growled, "I hate IVs almost as much as I hate cracked ribs." He pushed at the sheet and looked as if he was about to get up. "Where are my clothes?"

Bridgette stopped him. "Luke, stay down, boy!" she said, grinning. "I told you Tony's coming around and should be okay in a couple of days. The IV is necessary because you were severely dehydrated from the exertion of carrying Tony. That's the second liter. I'm sure they'll discontinue the IV as soon as it's finished infusing." She glanced behind her to where Claire was still standing in the doorway. Looking back at Luke she said, "The staff is avoiding coming in here, because of your lovely demeanor, so I brought someone to improve your mood."

As she was talking, Luke's eyes cut to the door and pinned Claire. His face colored, changing from pale to red, and he glanced down to where he'd pushed back the sheet and quickly re-covered his legs.

"Hey there." He smiled at her and held out his hand. "How're you doing? I'd get up, but…um…they've taken my clothes." He gave her a funny, slightly embarrassed look.

With a sob, she ran to the bed. Carefully avoiding his injured right side and working around the IV line and EKG leads, she knelt beside him. Claire threw her arms around his neck and whispered, "Luke… I'm sorry…I'm so sorry… I love you." She kissed his cheek and held him tightly.

Luke cautiously pulled her into an embrace. He actually chuckled. "I'm guessing you didn't mean you're sorry that you love me."

"Uh…I'm going to check on Tony," Bridgette mumbled and departed, closing the door behind her.

Claire giggled as she buried her face in his neck. "No. I'm sorry that you're hurt and Tony's hurt, and that it was all because of me." She pulled away and studied his smiling eyes, which were now more green than brown. Her voice quieted to a whisper. "The other, though— You're wonderful. I love you."

"I know," he whispered back. He pulled her toward him again and kissed her temple. "I love you, too." She ran her hands across his face and stroked his hair. He stopped her hands with his free one and lightly kissed her knuckles. "Hey, I've been lying here thinking, and I have a question. It's kind of important." He studied her expression carefully. "Well, uh, how would you feel about a destination wedding?"

Claire sat back so abruptly she almost fell off the bed. "Destination wedding?" She went from pale to pink to pale again in only a few seconds.

"Yeah. How about Hawaii? I was thinking that Hawaii would be a great place to get married. What do you think?"

Claire searched his face and saw humor but also something else—something deep, something serious, something bordering on desperate. Longing and need were interspersed with love.

Claire blinked. She bit her lower lip and stared at him. "Um… Is that a proposal?"

"Yes." He gave her a small smile and kissed her hand again. "I know it's a poor effort. I don't have a ring and can't get on my knees." His words softened and his smile faded. "But I promise no one will ever love you more than I do." He gently cradled her face in his hands. "I want to be with you, make a life with you, have children with you…"

Tears clouded her eyes, but her lips turned up at the corners. "I've never been to Hawaii. I think it must be the perfect place for a wedding." She leaned forward and touched his mouth with hers, once, twice and then sank into a deep kiss.

When she pulled back, his smile was sweet. "I'll take that as a 'yes,' then."

"Yes," she laughed. "Yes. Yes."

Luke held her a while, stroking her back as they relished the quiet contentment after their grueling day. After a few minutes he pushed her away a little so he could see her face. "This is kind of fast and we still need to talk about some important things." He took her hand in his and interlaced their fingers.

She sat back and replied, "What things?"

"The nightmares or night terrors or whatever you want to call them… I don't know… I hope I can control…"

"Luke, I told you, we'll work it out. I trust you. I trust you not to hurt me. I've done some research and in most cases the nightmares decrease with time. I promise, I'm not concerned…"

He looked relieved, but the worry still clouded his eyes. He swallowed. "I'll talk to the counselor next week, and we'll see what he says…"

She rewarded him with a smile and a kiss. "That's a very good idea. I'm sure he'll reassure you that nightmares are pretty common and will resolve. Is there anything else? You said 'things'."

He studied her face, seemingly lost in her eyes. "Well, yes. Another big one…"

She frowned. "What?"

"Texas." His lips thinned a little and the

worry was back. "How do you feel about living in Texas?"

Claire sat back and crossed her legs, getting more comfortable on the bed. She smiled brightly. "Well, I guess I'll need to get used to the idea, won't I? Especially since that's where my husband-to-be lives and where I assume he'll be working... What are you smiling at?

"What you said. I liked it."

"What did I say?"

"My husband." He caressed her face, stroking her cheek gently. He looked enormously relieved. "Are you sure? It's okay to leave your parents? Your work? Your doctorate?"

"My parents will understand. And about my work and school—I can finish my degree from anywhere—I'm in Korea now for goodness' sake. And I'm sure I can find a position in Texas." She blinked and her smile faded. "Unfortunately, they have sick children there, too."

Luke's eyes filled suddenly. "Thank you. I promise I'll make you happy."

She smiled and kissed him again. Sitting back up, she said, "There is one other very significant problem we'll have to address, though."

"Oh. And what's that?"

"Cowboys…" She shook her head and gave him a pained expression. "I don't think I can ever be a Cowboys fan."

He laughed as she'd hoped he would. "I guess we're going to have to have a mixed marriage then. It'll probably work out all right until we have children… We'll have to split the kids between us—half Packers half Cowboys."

She chuckled and hugged him again. "I guess we can work that out when the time comes!"

A knock at the door had Claire scrambling to her feet. Luke's glare was almost comical. "Come in," he replied grumpily.

Jessica entered followed by Detective Kang and Captain Choi. "Hey, guys. Great news! I just saw Tony. He's awake and alert and mad as a hornet." Her smile was brilliant. "Isn't it wonderful?"

Claire clasped Luke's hand and had to blink back tears of relief. Luke's jaw clenched as he, too, fought to contain his emotions. After a few seconds he managed to respond. "Whew! Okay, yes. That's fantastic!" He turned to stare at the two policemen and said, "Would you all mind leaving for a minute. Claire, find the nurse and have her bring me my clothes. I'm not having a conversation with anyone about anything official until I'm dressed."

"Yes, Lieutenant." Claire couldn't contain her smile. "I'll find your nurse right now."

CHAPTER EIGHTEEN

TEN MINUTES LATER, the group re-entered Luke's room and found him dressed and minus the IV line, which he'd convinced the nurse to remove. He was sitting on the edge of the bed and pulled Claire down beside him, leaving the lone chair for Jessica. The policemen remained standing.

Detective Kang took notes as the trio recounted the events of the afternoon. When they finished their narrative, Luke frowned at the captain and said, "You already knew about Lee Min-sik, didn't you?"

Captain Choi nodded. "Yes." He glanced at the detective, who explained.

"Yesterday, after kidnap attempt, we find man in emergency room—Mr. Jin-hee Ji—with broken hand." Detective Kang's smile was sly. "Hospital call us and I interview."

Captain Choi picked up the account.

"The detective did a very thorough interrogation. After several hours of intense discussions, we learned the names of the accomplices. We sent officers to pick them up, also for interrogation. There were four men all together, and by the time we had them all in custody, they were ready to tell us everything."

He looked pleased with their efforts and continued to explain. "Two of the men—Jin-hee Ji and Ra-won Kim—were the original pair who attacked Miss Olsen at the Medical Center. Kim and a man named Min-a Shinn attacked you, Miss Tyson. A fourth man, Ja-ok Kim, drove the car when the pair from the hospital tried to kidnap Miss Olsen again. That driver, along with Ra-won Kim, tried to kill you today." He gave a shrug. "Ja-ok Kim was badly injured when the car ran off the mountain road. He will likely not make it."

Detective Kang continued. "They were all hired by Lee Min-sik. Mr. Lee is human resource director for Taekung Industries—large Korean company."

Captain Choi nodded. "After all four assassins admitted they were hired by the same man, we sent police to the Taekung offices to arrest Mr. Lee." He shook his head. "Mr. Lee knew the police were coming. Rather than be arrested, he took the elevator to the top of the building." He held Luke's eyes for a minute before turning to Claire. "He jumped."

Claire gasped. "Oh, no." She stood and walked to the window. "When did this happen?"

"Late this afternoon. About an hour ago. We were informed of his death right before Ms. Tyson called us. Mr. Lee knew his efforts to do away with you were not successful. He would be put in prison— probably for many years. He could not live with the dishonor."

Claire struggled to comprehend all that she'd been told. She struggled to understand her own feelings. Her uncle—her birth mother's brother—had tried repeatedly to kill her. Despite being a victim of his evil intent, she felt no hate or animosity. Indeed, she had no feeling for or about him at all. She wasn't glad he was dead, but neither was she sorry. She was sim-

ply ambivalent—and incredibly relieved.
A thought occurred to her.

"Did he have a family?"

"Yes. He has wife, two children. Boy
and girl—younger than you," answered
Detective Kang.

"What will happen to them?"

"They have money from grandparents,
but will have to make reparations to the
company for loss of face. Very sad."

"Then I'm sorry for them," Claire said.

They talked a few more minutes and finally the policemen were ready to leave.
They shook hands with Luke and Jessica and turned to Claire. Detective Kang
shook her hand and then Captain Choi offered his, saying, "Miss Olsen, I regret all
that's happened to you while you were in
Seoul. I would assure you that our country
is safe, but I don't know if you will believe
me." He looked forlorn. "I have removed
the hold on your passport and you may
leave anytime. I hope you will come back
some day, so you can see that our country—your country—is a lovely one."

"Thank you, Captain, for all your help
and for coming in person to explain what

happened. I will be leaving soon—" she glanced at Luke "—but who knows, we may be back some day." She smiled and bid the men goodbye.

AFTER THE POLICEMEN departed, Jessica, Luke and Claire sat for a few minutes to let the information sink in. Then they looked in on Tony and were vastly relieved when they found him sitting up in bed, wearing a hospital gown and looking annoyed. A white bandage circled his head, holding a bulky dressing in place over his right eyebrow and much of his forehead. His right eye was almost swollen shut.

Jessica took his hand. "Matching black eyes!" she murmured. Her smile was wry. "We're quite a pair, aren't we?"

His scowl turned into a half grin. "Hey, I win. I have function of both my arms."

"Yeah, so? I don't have a concussion."

"Your eye?" Claire asked. "Was there any damage?"

Tony shrugged and shook his head. "The jury's still out on that one. I have a little blurring right now, but there's hope it'll be fine." He sighed and looked comically forlorn. "The CT scan indicated there might be a small brain bleed." He glanced at Claire and Luke. "I have to stay a day or so for another scan… I hate hospitals."

They all laughed with relief knowing just how bad it might have been.

IN THE END, Luke was able to convince the head E.D. doctor that since he had a private nurse, he didn't need to stay in the hospital. With that development, Jessica went home with Bridgette, while Claire accompanied Luke to his apartment.

It was after eight when they finally arrived. Both were exhausted after the long and eventful day.

"Okay, Luke, I promised the major I would give you a pain pill and make sure you went straight to bed," Claire informed her patient as she closed and locked the front door.

Luke caught her in his arms—carefully. He gave her a quick kiss and started to let go, but he couldn't quite make himself do it. In a breath, he was holding her tightly, unable to let go. Finally, he pulled back.

She kissed him sweetly. "I wanted to ask

you something... Were you serious about Hawaii? Next week? I mean, about getting married next week?"

"Yes, I'm serious." He stroked her cheek and gave a slight frown, but he quickly replaced it with a half smile. "If you would rather wait—if you want to have a big wedding at your home...that would be fine, too."

She knew that he meant it—he would do whatever she wanted. A big wedding in Minnesota sometime in the future or a small wedding next week in Hawaii—he would let her choose. His willingness to defer to her wishes meant the world to her, and she knew without question what she wanted.

"Luke, I want to marry you as soon as we can work it out. A Hawaiian wedding—and honeymoon—sounds like a fairy tale." She felt her smile fade. "There may be a problem, though. My parents really don't have the money—to travel to Hawaii, I mean. I don't know if they could come... I suppose we could get married next week and then have another ceremony for them in Minnesota later on..."

He smoothed the crease from between her eyes. "Don't worry, Mary Claire. I'll take care of their expenses."

"No, Luke. I can't ask you to do that. That would be expensive and it's not fair to you. I mean, the bride is supposed to pay for the wedding." She shrugged and felt her cheeks flush. "I don't have a lot of savings because I've been paying for all my tuition without taking loans. That's pretty much eaten into my savings."

He caught her by the hand and pulled her toward to sofa. "Claire, sit down." His voice had grown serious. "There's another discussion we need to have." Carefully he sat beside her and clasped her hand again.

Her heart rate climbed and she looked at him worriedly. "Luke, you're starting to make me nervous. Is something wrong?"

He sighed and looked toward the computers as if for inspiration. "This is oddly harder than I thought it would be. Okay, here goes." He captured her eyes with his. "About fifty years ago, they discovered oil on my grandfather Carter's cotton farm. There was a lot of it."

Claire sat back and blinked her eyes in

confusion. "So what are you telling me?" She scooted a little away from him.

"Well, my grandparents got pretty rich… Okay, really rich…" He gave a funny little half smile and then continued. "Eventually, those wells mostly played out. The family was still rich, but the income had dwindled. Then about fifteen years ago my dad started re-engineering all of the wells on the Carter land. My brother Matt joined him about ten years ago and then Mark. Long story short, they've moved way beyond just developing on the Carter land and now are one of the larger engineering companies involved with hydraulic fracturing in the Permian Basin." He played nervously with her fingers. "John, my younger brother, just graduated with his MBA and is expanding the business operation in Houston. I'm joining the company with the intent of using my computer skills in both the engineering and business sides. In my spare time, I've been developing a computer program to be used in the fracking process. It's designed to identify the best prospective areas for production to lessen any potential environmental impact.

Anyway, we've talked about it—my dad and brothers… They can use me—well, us—either in Houston or in Midland—it doesn't really matter where. It's kind of up to you…"

She stared at him. "Fracking. You said something about fracking before. I didn't follow you then. And you said something about your fiancée wanting your money. I didn't get it then, either." Her lips turned down a bit and her forehead creased. "So your family has a successful oil company, and you're rich."

He gave her a funny frown. "Well, yes… I guess that's pretty much it."

"Oh." She looked down and then away from him. "Well, okay. I'm not really sure what I'm supposed to say now… I guess— um—wow, that's wonderful."

"Claire, honey, is something wrong?"

"No, of course not… I don't think… You just took me by surprise, that's all." She stood and walked toward the window. "I never thought a lot about money. I mean, I've always had enough. I've helped my parents when I could and worked my way through school so they wouldn't be burdened. It never occurred to me, I guess, to want to be—um, rich."

She studied him then and something belatedly occurred to her. "It doesn't matter to you, either, does it?" She smiled in wonder. "You did this—" she swept her hand around the room in an inclusive gesture "—even though you were wealthy. You became a naval officer, living in sometimes dire conditions and putting your life on the line for probably a fraction of your normal monthly income."

It was his turn to look uncomfortable. "Don't give me too much credit. I told you, I did it initially because I had this wild idea that I wanted to fly fighter jets and land on aircraft carriers, and that was the only way to do it. It just didn't work out like I'd intended."

"No, but you stayed because it was important."

"Yes, I guess I did. But now, I want to go home and I want you to come with me."

"You want me to pick Midland or Houston? It truly doesn't matter. Wherever makes the most sense and where we can spend the most time together is what

I want." She threw her arms around him again. "You're stuck with me now."

A COUPLE OF hours later, Claire was at the computer. She had completed a long note to her parents trying to explain all that had happened in the past two weeks. Earlier she and Luke had called them via Skype to invite them on a vacation in Hawaii. The only catch was the short notice and the fact that they'd be marrying off their only daughter. After their initial surprise—and once they'd seen Claire's joy—they happily agreed.

After the phone call, Luke finally prepared for bed. Claire gave him his pain medication, hoping it would eliminate much of his discomfort, allowing him to sleep. She smiled as she tucked him in. As she was about to leave, he pulled her back to sit next to him. "One more kiss," he murmured, already starting to get drowsy.

She complied with a soft kiss and then slid down to lovingly touch her lips to the bandage on his sore ribs. "I was recently told that will make it better." She smiled sweetly. "I know it worked for me."

He groaned and pulled her back into his arms. "Okay, soon, really soon, you're going to be staying with me. I love you…"

"Yes, I know." She smiled shyly. "I love you, too."

She turned to go, but he stopped her at the door. "Claire." His voice had lost its playfulness. "I just took that pain pill so I'll probably sleep hard. Promise me—I need you to promise me—that under no circumstance will you come in here if you hear me having a nightmare."

She considered his request for a moment and then shook her head. Walking back to the bed, she took his hand. "No, Luke. I'm not going to promise that."

He sat up in bed, looking alarmed at first and then angry. Before he could comment she said, "I love you. I don't think I could ever *not* respond if I heard you cry out—whether you were asleep or not."

"Claire, we've had this discussion before. I could hurt you." He emphasized each word.

"No, I don't think so. I know what to expect now, and so do you. Even subconsciously, even asleep, I think you would know me." She gripped his hand and stared into his eyes, willing him to understand. "Luke, I won't stay away. You're just going to have to trust me like I trust you."

It dawned on him then. With her declaration, Luke realized that while he'd lost the battle, nonetheless, he had won. A slender, brave, generous, half-Korean half-American young woman with beautiful eyes had earned his absolute trust.

"I love you, very much," he answered. Feeling the effects of the drug, he kissed her hand then lay back down and went to sleep.

AFTER SENDING THE NOTE to her parents, Claire spent a while looking at wedding dresses online. She was about to sign off from the computer, eager to get ready for bed, when she heard the sound of someone at the apartment's front door. Her head jerked up when the knob turned and the door opened. A man with dark auburn hair stood there.

With mounting concern, she watched as he reached down to pick up a bag. He straightened then stopped short when he saw her staring at him with a frightened expression. Surprised, the man took a step back and glanced at the apartment number, as if making sure he was at the correct place. Reassured on that account, he turned back to her.

The intruder was quite tall and appeared to be athletic. He was dressed in dark blue coveralls that identified him as a military man.

"Uh, hello," he said. "Um, I live here… I'm Brad Littlejohn." He peered into the room. His expressive green eyes looked worried. "Is Luke around?"

Claire responded with a choking laugh that turned into a giggle. "Hi, Brad. I'm Claire. It's nice to finally meet you." She stepped forward and held out her hand. "You missed a lot while you were away. Let me get us both some coffee, and I'll fill you in."

EPILOGUE

Six years later

"Seoul hasn't changed much," Claire remarked as she watched the city through the window of the taxi.

"Yeah, traffic is still bad and the air is still hazy," Luke grumbled.

Claire grinned at him. She understood that Luke's grouchiness was due to lack of sleep. The flight from Houston was more than fifteen hours, and it had been nearly impossible for him to rest, even in business class.

"You can take a nap when we get to the hotel," she said cheerily.

"Maybe just a short one—I know you're anxious to meet her." He pulled his lovely wife into the circle of his arms and buried his face in her hair. "What time did you tell Mrs. Lee that we'd be there?"

"Not until two this afternoon." She glanced at her watch. "About four hours from now." She sighed, snuggled closer to Luke and gave him a warm kiss. Hopefully the taxi driver wasn't too shocked by their behavior. "Thank you for doing this for me. I know you were—well, are—hesitant. But I know in my heart it's the right thing."

He held her tightly. "We've talked this through many times. I'm not doing it for you. It's for us. And it's for the boys, too."

"But you're less certain than I am…"

"I don't see how I could possibly love anyone as much as I love the boys. You know that. We've talked about it."

She just smiled and kissed him on the corner of his mouth. "Luke, I know you. I'm not worried."

They rode in silence for a little while, but she was so excited she couldn't sit still. "I just wish we could have brought Sam and Eli."

"Honey, that flight was hard enough on you and me—well, at least on me. You seem to have managed pretty well. But imagine what it would have been like with a two-year-old and a four-year-old."

He shuddered. "I don't want to even consider the horror of that prospect!"

She giggled. "I suppose you're right. I just hope they'll be good for your parents."

He chuckled. "Me, too. What time is it in Midland? We probably need to Skype as soon as we get to the hotel so we can check on them."

An hour later, Claire used her iPad to set up a video call from their hotel room. First they talked to Luke's mother and got a report on what all the boys had done so far. They talked to four-year-old Samuel for a few minutes before he wandered off to play with the family pets. Two-year-old Elijah, they learned, was already in bed for the night. Both had been very good for their grandparents. Claire and Luke had been told not to worry and to have a wonderful time in Seoul.

While she was getting ready for the upcoming meeting, Claire reflected on the past six years. They'd had a small, lovely wedding on the island of Kauai. Despite the short notice, all of Luke's family had been able to attend, and the Llewellyns turned the trip into a homecoming celebration for their middle son, a wedding and a family vacation.

Other than the Llewellyns and Claire's parents, the only other guests were Tony, Jessica, Bridgette and Brad. Tony had nearly recovered and Jessica's face was bruise-free, but the cast on her arm would remain another few weeks. Claire smiled to herself as she recalled that within six months, they, too, had married, and the following year Tony had surprised everyone by deciding to leave the Marines. They moved to Southern California, where Tony started a security company and Jessica joined the faculty of UCLA. Their work, along with their two little girls, kept them very busy, but they'd been able to meet last year as Luke and Claire took little Sam to Disneyland.

Likewise, Bridgette and Brad were able to make the trip to Hawaii to be a part of the wedding. They insisted that Luke and Claire reciprocate, making them promise to travel from Texas to Missouri the same summer for their own wedding. Six years later, Brad was now an Air Force flight instructor and they lived in Colorado. Their son, Brian—to no one's surprise—was a darling redhead. He was Eli's age—just past two. Bridgette was pregnant again, this time hoping for a girl, who would undoubtedly also have red hair.

As predicted, Luke's mother—Sarah—was crazy about Claire. What hadn't been predicted was how well Luke's parents got along with Claire's parents. During the week of activities before and after the wedding, the Llewellyns and the Olsens became fast friends. After the wedding, they all remained on Kauai while the newlyweds chartered a plane and left to spend a week in a rented beach house on the relatively quiet island of Molokai.

Claire's parents further surprised her by moving to central Texas when her father retired a few years later. They said they wanted to finally get away from the cold Minnesota winters, but no one was really fooled. They wanted to be near their grandchildren. They had settled in very well and eventually adjusted to the Texas summers. However, the Olsens remained die-hard Green Bay Packers fans, which led to considerably raucous visits during football season.

After considerable deliberation, Claire and Luke decided to live in Houston. Luke split his time—working from home several days each week and from the downtown offices that were headed by his brother John the rest of the time. Claire had finished her doctorate and worked for several years at the M.D. Anderson Cancer Institute, implementing a playroom program based on the one in Seoul, to provide comprehensive care for children with cancer. She worked only part-time after the birth of little Samuel, mostly as a consultant. After Elijah's birth, she cut back on her work even more but would occasionally take speaking engagements.

She smiled with pride and pleasure when she thought of their two sons. Samuel had her black hair. He was an easygoing and sweet little boy who loved to play with computers, just like his father. Then, two years later, along came Elijah. Eli weighed nearly ten pounds at birth, and from the beginning, he was all Llewellyn. Her second son was destined—according to his paternal grandfather—to be a football player. His birth, however, had been difficult for Claire, and she'd suffered complications. Her obstetrician had been adamant that it would be dangerous for her to have any more pregnancies.

Claire was devastated. She adored her little boys and loved being a mother, but her family didn't feel complete. She wanted—she *needed*—more children.

Luke had expressed reluctance when she told him about her desire, but he eventually agreed with her plan. Over the next year, she made a number of contacts, and together they endured multiple interviews and talked to a score of different people. Finally, they were here, and she was nearly overcome with joy.

IN THE BEGINNING, Luke had tried to share his concerns with Claire. During both of her pregnancies, from the moment he'd learned that Claire was expecting, he was ecstatic. Luke was totally in love with the babies he didn't even know yet. He loved them because they were part of Claire and part of himself. Then when they were born and he held them in his arms, he fell in love all over again. Now, faced with the prospect of adoption, he harbored apprehension that bordered on fear that he wouldn't be able to feel the same love for someone else's child.

But Luke would do anything for Claire, so he'd endured the interviews and the visits and the forms and the discussions with lawyers. And now he'd traveled back to Seoul with her to pick up the child—a little girl—to take her home.

He watched Claire get dressed for the interview and the introduction to the baby and he said a silent prayer: *Please let me not disappoint Claire. Please let me pull this off...*

"Okay, I'm ready." She was radiant. Beaming, she smoothed her skirt and asked, "Do I look okay?"

"Claire, she's six months old. She won't care how you look." He managed a smile and kissed her lovingly on the temple.

As they got into the cab, Luke's stomach was churning. He wasn't sure he could go through with it. His smiles and cheerful demeanor were forced and awkward, but with her excitement, Claire didn't seem to notice.

The cab finally dropped them off at the Asian Social Welfare Agency. Luke's edginess was making him queasy. Nevertheless, he composed himself and was able to walk up the steps and enter the building.

Mrs. Lee, who seemed not to have aged in six years, met them in the waiting area. Luke managed to greet her, smile and responded appropriately to her questions and comments.

Mrs. Lee seemed genuinely delighted to see Luke again, but her attention quickly turned to Claire, because of the peculiar situation. It was almost unheard of for an adoptee to return as an adoptive parent. With a great deal of enthusiasm, Mrs. Lee called all of the workers over to meet the couple, and Luke was subjected to a host of well wishers, who said overly polite things to him in Korean. He forced himself to be gracious and feign pleasure because it was important to Claire.

Finally, it was time. "Let us go meet your little angel," Mrs. Lee said.

Claire was glowing with anticipation as

she grabbed Luke's hand and smiled into his eyes. Once again he said a quick prayer for strength as they were shown into one of the small family rooms that they'd viewed six years ago. "Please sit," Mrs. Lee said. "I will only be a moment."

For several minutes, they waited in silence. Luke's heart was beating erratically and his palms were sweating. He badly wanted to flee. At last the door opened and Mrs. Lee returned with the baby. He and Claire stood.

At first glance, she was the most beautiful baby Luke had ever seen. With a muffled sob, Claire held out her arms to take the tiny, six-month-old girl. "Hello, little one," she cooed. "We're going to name you Rachel." Tears flowed down her cheeks, and her voice cracked. "I'm your new Mommy." She kissed the baby's temple and continued to talk. "This is your new Daddy. I know he's kind of big and seems scary, but he's really wonderful. Together, we're going to take very good care of you."

The baby's soft black hair was surprisingly long for an infant and had lovely waves. She looked at Claire with interest, and although she didn't understand English, she seemed to comprehend the loving tone in which the words were uttered. Tentatively she smiled.

"Oh, my goodness," Claire exclaimed. Still cradling the child, she sat down on the small sofa and continued to talk to the baby sweetly, quietly, lovingly.

Luke had been standing to the side, unable to move any nearer. Finally, drawn by an unseen force, he came over to sit on the far side of the sofa. Then he looked, really looked at the baby and saw...

Her eyes.

He was stunned. "Oh, dear Lord," he whispered. "Mary Claire, her eyes—they're like yours." After a while, he realized he was holding his breath as he stared at the child. He exhaled and thrust his hands in his pockets.

The baby's eyes were not an exact replica of Claire's, but the similarity was striking. They were an unusual dark blue, but the child had the same anomaly in which an outer section of both irises was a light amber color. The baby's eyes, like Claire's, revealed that she was mixed race and therefore not adoptable by most Korean families.

Hesitantly, he leaned over, touching her lightly on her plump little cheek with his finger. When he did, she looked at him directly and smiled. Her happy little smile revealed two tiny teeth and she reached her arms toward him. Language wasn't needed to understand what she wanted.

At that moment—that very moment—Luke's concerns and fears evaporated like vapor on a hot, sunny day. They were replaced by something warm and simple and enduring. Unable to do otherwise, he gathered her into his arms.

He closed his eyes tightly and murmured a brief prayer of thanks as he savored the moment. He kissed her downy head. "Hi, Rachel," he said. Luke's big hands were infinitely gentle as he held her. "We're going to take you home to Texas. You've got two big brothers who are going to help take care of you." His voice was gravelly and broken when he whispered, "I'm your Daddy."

His eyes were filled with tears when they met Claire's. He should have known.

After all these years with her, he should have known that giving and receiving love could be so simple and so easy.

He kissed the baby again and smiled at Claire. "Let's go home."

* * * * *

LARGER-PRINT BOOKS!

GET 2 FREE
LARGER-PRINT NOVELS
PLUS 2 FREE
MYSTERY GIFTS

Love Inspired®

Larger-print novels are now available...

LILPDIR13R

ReaderService.com

Manage your account online!

- Review your order history
- Manage your payments
- Update your address

> ### We've designed the Harlequin® Reader Service website just for you.

Enjoy all the features!

- Reader excerpts from any series
- Respond to mailings and special monthly offers
- Discover new series available to you
- Browse the Bonus Bucks catalog
- Share your feedback

Visit us at:
ReaderService.com